Say Yes, Baby

Geneva Gordon

DDP
DEEP DESIRES PRESS
Winnipeg, Canada

Developmental editor: Craig Gibb
Proofreader: Margaret Larson

Published May 2024 by Deep Desires Press, an imprint of Story Perfect Inc.

Deep Desires Press
PO Box 51053 Tyndall Park
Winnipeg, Manitoba R2X 3B0
Canada

Visit http://www.deepdesirespress.com for more scorching hot erotica and erotic romance.

Say Yes, Baby

PROLOGUE

This was what he had expected. This was the deal-breaker that Scott Benson threw on the table. This was his ace that was going to force Mickey Finn to cough up another five million to close this deal.

Mickey leaned back in his chair, steepling his fingers while he looked Scott Benson in the eyes. The fact that Mickey hadn't blanched or gasped or even so much as flared his nostrils had Scott a little perturbed.

What Scott Benson didn't know, but should have known, was that Mickey Finn did his due diligence…and then some. He knew everything he needed to know about the property he had offered ten million for. Everything he needed to know and everything Scott Benson did not want him to know.

"I know about the other offer, Scott. But you are contractually bound to close this deal with me, at the price offered, not one penny more, but perhaps a few million less." Mickey watched as Scott processed that last statement. "I've done my due diligence. I know about the City's claim for back taxes. I don't know how you managed to keep that off the tax roll but I know about it. Three million in back taxes, five hundred thousand in arrears and penalties, another two hundred thousand in legal fees and processing fees to have this taken care of. Let's just call it an even four million off the purchase price."

Scott looked at his lawyer who was sitting next to him.

"Mr. Finn, that's an extra three hundred thousand that you have tacked on," Scott's mouthpiece said. "We are looking at a possible reduction of only three point seven million for a property that is well worth the original ten million offered."

"That may be so, but your client accepted my ten million dollar offer. As it stands, that property is no longer worth ten million with the taxes and penalties levied against it. It will be worth more, much more, once my development is complete but that is my business, not something your client should profit from. About the extra three hundred thousand, that would be the cost of my annoyance of having to deal with this and Mr. Benson's cost to avoid the damage caused by the negative publicity that would result from his attempt to pull one over on me."

Mickey stared at Scott. Scott broke eye contact first. He leaned over to his lawyer. They held a short, whispered conversation. Scott straightened up, nodded his head, and said, "Okay, reduction of three point seven million." He held out his hand.

Mickey looked at his hand but didn't take it. "Four million, Scott. If you had been fair about this, we would have closed at ten million but it's the price of your duplicity. Take the deal. I have a lien registered against the property. I won't discharge it. You'll have to spend another million in court to get rid of it. Everyone will know about the tax matter. If this is the way you want to go, then you will only clear two million by the time this is finished with. Take my deal."

Scott's body tensed, his eyes narrowed, he shot a look of pure hatred at Mickey. "Finn," he barked.

The door to the boardroom opened. Talia, Mickey's assistant, leaned into the room. All eyes turned to her. She surely felt the tension in the room but calmly met Mickey's eyes. "I've got that call you have been waiting for," she said before closing the door.

Mickey stood. "I've got to take this, gentlemen, if you'll excuse me." He quickly strode out the boardroom, down the hall to his office, and picked up the phone.

"Toby," he smiled as he spoke.

"Bro! I'm going to be there next week. Monday. But only for like a day and a half. Clear your calendar, tycoon."

"Talia," he called to her at her desk outside of his office, "clear Monday and Tuesday next week. I'm going to be out."

She looked up at him, nodded, and turned her attention back to her screen.

"Done. When are you going to get here?"

"Monday, early. We'll be at the hotel crashing. Then the arena for set up and sound check around one. Plan on coming for about five. Concert starts at seven. We'll hang out until then. The guys are looking forward to seeing you, too. It's been too long, bro."

"Too long, Toby. But I have to go, I'm just about to close a deal and I can't let this guy sit for too long or he'll get a chance to relax."

Toby laughed. "Go get him, killer. Love ya, bro. See you next week."

"You can count on it."

Mickey hung up the phone. Smiling, he left his office and headed back to the boardroom. By the time he opened the door, the smile was gone and Scott Benson was ready to sign the papers.

CHAPTER 1
Mickey

Tony, Mickey's driver dropped him off at the arena. "It's going to be a long night," he said as he stepped out of the car. "Don't wait. I'll get home on my own."

You don't just casually walk into the arena where Temptation is playing two hours before the concert and expect to get in. Mickey was met by a security guard who blocked his path as soon as he came in the door. The guy was imposing; tall and heavily muscled. Still, he had to look up to meet Mickey's eyes.

"Mickey Finn," he said.

The guard nodded. He pulled a lanyard out of his back pocket and handed it to Mickey. He nodded his head toward a door to the left. "Through there. You'll hear 'em."

Mickey put the lanyard over his head and headed in the direction the security guard had indicated. He went through the designated door into a long concrete hallway and, yeah, he could hear them. A smile spread across his face.

He had always been the "money man" of the family. Business always made sense to him. He always knew how to take a dollar and turn it into two dollars, then five dollars and so on. He'd worked and hustled since he first started working at one thing or the other from the tender age of ten. By the time he was fifteen he was the owner of a small weedy patch of land on the outskirts of the city. When he graduated high school at eighteen, he paid for his entire university education by selling that weedy patch of land which was standing in the way of city expansion.

When he graduated university, he liquidated investments and sold some other land to open his development company. Within five years he was a multi-millionaire. At this point in his life, he was a billionaire.

His brother, Toby, didn't get it. He didn't understand long-term investment, speculation, or land development. What Toby did get was music. He understood how to write a song—words and music. He was also a master of having a good time.

When Toby was fifteen, he had assembled his band. He was lead singer, Marcus on bass, Silvio on drums, and LeShawn on guitar. They started in Toby's garage and, as long as they quit by ten p.m. the neighbors didn't complain or call the cops.

Their first gigs were a high school lunch dance, some community club dances, and a couple private parties. When the guys hit eighteen and could legally get into bars, their name grew. They went to Mickey for a loan to upgrade their equipment and buy a van. Within five years they had repaid their debt and were touring.

No one had to explain marketing or promotion to Toby. He got it. A small local band became an internet sensation thanks to Toby's promotions, some of which, through sheer dumb luck, didn't land them in jail. It wasn't long before they had their first recording contract. That was ten years ago.

They were still together; they were still popular with a dedicated fan base. They all relocated to the west coast, closer to their studio, their agent, their label. They were on their North American tour. Now, they were here, back home where it all started.

Mickey followed the noise down the hall, past doors on the left and the right, around a corner and, finally, he arrived at the door behind which all the noise was coming from. He put his hand on the doorknob when the song ended and he entered the room. All eyes turned to him and for a second, no one moved. Then Toby jumped up from the couch he had been lounging on, he strode across the room and took Mickey into a bear hug. LeShawn yelled out "Money in the house." Marcus whooped.

Toby released Mickey. LeShawn grabbed his hand and pulled him in for a man hug. "S'up, Money Man." He laughed.

"Too long, Money," Marcus said as he clasped Mickey's hand.

"It's good to see you guys again." Mickey smiled. "Hey, where's Silvio?"

"Appendix got him," Toby said. "He's MIA for a couple months."

"Who's on drums then?" Mickey asked.

Toby's eyebrows lifted and he nodded to the corner behind Mickey.

Mickey turned and there she was. There was a vision,

wrapped in a white terry robe sitting cross legged on a couch. Her eyes were closed. There were buds in her ears. She had a pair of drumsticks in her hands and she was drumming to whatever she was listening to. She was slim and dainty in appearance, short black hair artfully messy. Good God!

Mickey turned back to Toby.

"Parker Chen," Toby said. "Our label sent her. She's a studio musician. Man, she rocks. There's nothing she can't play. We have her until Silvio gets back."

"Umm," Mickey said.

"Yeah, she's in the zone. Nothing exists right now. She'll come out of it when it's time to play, no worries, bro. C'mon, let's get you liquored up." He slapped Mickey on the back and handed him a bottle of Jack.

Mickey tipped the bottle up and felt the liquor burn down his throat as he watched Parker. This evening just got a lot more interesting.

$$$

Mickey couldn't remember the last time he had been so relaxed. The guys were just as funny as when they were fifteen. Still playing the same gags, working off the same stale jokes. He couldn't remember when he'd laughed this much.

A guy poked his head in the room and shouted out "Fifteen minutes!" before closing the door. The guys slowly stopped what they were doing before standing and filing out the door. Mickey stood, leaning against the wall watching

Parker. Shouldn't someone let her know it was time to go? He was debating what to do when her hands stopped moving.

She put her drumsticks down, unfolded her legs, leaned forward and grabbed her ankles and stood, pushing her forehead into her knees. She released her ankles, turned her back to Mickey and stretched. She stood on her toes and pushed her arms out above her head. She took the buds out of her ears, undid her robe, and turned around.

She was in a tiny white bikini, firm breasts covered by white triangles. Her stomach was flat, her abs defined. The bottoms were small, just large enough to cover what needed to be covered and not much else. She wore black Doc Martens, the laces done halfway up.

She saw Mickey immediately. She picked up her drumsticks and looked at his face briefly before dropping her eyes down over his chest, down over his hips, down over his legs to his feet, then back up, stopping at his crotch. She smiled a little smile and then continued back up to his face. She met his eyes and walked toward him.

She stopped in front of him and put her hand on his chest. His muscles contracted under her hand. Mickey was frozen watching her, not knowing what she was going to do. She watched her hand as she trailed it down his T-shirt, momentarily stopping at his belt before… Mickey growled and grabbed her hand to stop whatever it was that she was intending to do.

She looked up and met his eyes again with a smirk on her lips, "I'll see much more of you later, Rod."

"Rod?"

"You're the stripper for later, aren't you? Hot Rod?"

Mickey snorted. "Definitely not, sweetheart."

"That's too bad. I would have given you a hundred dollars for a lap dance."

He bent down so he was on eye level with her. "The only way that is happening is if it's my lap and you're screaming my name."

He didn't know what he expected her to do or say to that. She really was so unlike any other woman he had ever met.

"Is that an offer?" Parker asked as she placed her hand on his cheek. She leaned forward and brushed her lips against his. "Too bad, Rod, I have to go."

She turned and left the room. Mickey remained where he was, bent forward to look into the eyes that were no longer in front of him. What. The. Fuck. Just. Happened?

CHAPTER 2
Mickey

The show was over, encores played, and they were massed together in the hall, surrounded by security and heading back to the room. Mickey's ears were still ringing. They filed into the room. The guys all picked up towels and started to wipe the sweat from their bodies, talking about the show, still high from an excellent performance.

Mickey stood apart from them all. He had a beer in his hand. He was waiting for the adrenaline to die down so they could plan what they were going to do next. The door to the room opened again and Parker came in. Her hair was plastered to her head, her body gleamed with sweat, her bikini was soaked. Toby picked up a towel and threw it at her. She caught it and wiped her body. Someone threw another towel at her. She caught it, opened it up and draped it over her head.

"I'm taking a shower," she announced. She picked up a gym bag on her way to the shower and closed the door behind her.

No one seemed to notice. The door to the room opened again and people started to stream in: roadies, women, their tour manager, more women. Mickey moved to stand in front of the bathroom door. The band was covered with women. Mickey smiled and took another sip from his bottle.

"Hey there," someone said.

Mickey looked down to find a very cute redhead looking up at him. "Hey yourself," he responded.

"You with the band?" she asked. She tilted her head to the side and licked her lips. She put her hand up to her neck and then trailed it down her chest, drawing attention to her low-cut blouse and the cleavage on display.

"No. My brother is."

"Really. Who's your brother?" She glanced at the band and then back at him.

"Toby."

"Really?" She held out her hand. "Melanie."

Mickey took her hand. "Mickey." He had a pretty good idea where this was headed but he would enjoy it while it lasted. She wasn't his type anyway.

"Why don't we go talk to your brother?" she suggested.

Just then the bathroom door behind him opened. Mickey looked over his shoulder to find Parker looking up at him. Her hair was damp, towel dried but not combed. She had changed into a T-shirt and ripped jean shorts.

"You know, you're really tall," she observed.

"Don't you ever comb your hair?" he asked.

"Do you hit your head on the door jamb when you enter or leave a room?" she asked, a serious look on her face.

He laughed and stood aside to give her space to pass him. She went across the room to get a beer. He watched as she walked away. She wore those shorts well. A roadie stopped her, starting up a conversation. He leaned toward her to speak into her ear, putting his hand on her elbow.

"Hello!"

Melanie stood with her hands on her hips. She clearly wasn't used to being ignored. She was a bit annoyed that he was looking at another woman while she was there.

Parker was still talking to the roadie. The guy slid his hand up to her shoulder, pulling her closer to him, then sliding his hand down her back to rest at her waist. Whatever was happening over there was about to be over. Mickey grabbed Melanie's wrist and pulled her along with him.

"Hey," she protested.

"You want to meet my brother, come with me."

He stopped beside Parker and the roadie.

"Parker," he said, pulling her attention away from the roadie toward him. "This is Melanie, she's a big fan."

Melanie stuttered. Parker looked at Melanie. The roadie walked away. Then Parker looked at him. Was that annoyance in her eyes? He couldn't tell and he didn't care.

"Always happy to meet a fan, Melanie," Parker said as she looked at the woman.

"Well, you know, you were great," Melanie said, looking awkward.

"Did you want me to autograph your tits?" Parker smirked.

"No!" She looked at Mickey. "You are such an asshole," she said as she stormed off.

"Not that big a fan, I think," Parker said.

"That's a shame. I thought she was."

"Hey, bro." Toby was at his side. "We're going for dinner, then a club. C'mon."

LeShawn joined them. "Why don't you take us to one of your fancy clubs, Money. Show us how the other half lives."

"Yeah, Money, you must know where we can get some prime pussy," Marcus said.

"Oh my God! Boys!" Parker huffed. "Have fun," she said as she turned away from them.

Mickey grabbed her wrist. "Don't you want dinner?"

Toby and LeShawn exchanged a look.

"I'm in for some food, Rod. I'll pass on the prime pussy. That's not my scene."

"Good to know," he said as he smiled at her.

Parker rolled her eyes.

$$$

Most of the guys had pushed themselves away from the table, leaning back in their chairs, digesting the excellent meal they had just consumed. They were in a private room in Mickey's members only club.

Parker was still eating. She had ordered a large meal and extra sides and was almost done. Their waiter appeared with another employee pushing a cart bearing numerous cakes, pies, slices, and other sweets.

"Can I interest anyone in dessert?" he asked as he passed his hand over the cart. "We have a delicious cherry cheesecake, a decadent chocolate torte enrobed with ganache, floating island, a refreshing lemon chiffon cake, and, of course, French vanilla ice cream drizzled with your choice of toppings. Or perhaps an aperitif?"

Several of the guys actually groaned.

"Not another bite, man," LeShawn said.

"I'm stuffed," Marcus said.

"Uncle," Toby moaned.

"Are you having dessert?" Parker asked, looking at Mickey.

"Do you want dessert?" he asked.

"I don't want to be the only one," she said.

"What do you want?" he asked.

"They all look good," she said as she looked at the cart. "I can't resist a good cheesecake. I love chocolate, though. Can't say I wouldn't have the lemon cake either."

Fuck, could she be any cuter? Mickey couldn't seem to take his eyes off her. Finally, he said, "She'll have the cheesecake, I'll have the chocolate torte, and a piece of the lemon cake for the table. Coffee anyone?" He counted the nods and the hands being raised. "Okay, coffee for everyone."

The waiter was back fifteen minutes later with the coffee and cake. Parker dug into her cheesecake with gusto. Mickey was talking to Toby when out of the corner of his eye he noticed her fork sneak onto his plate and take a bit of his chocolate cake. Toby smirked and nodded his head in acknowledgement that, yes, this was actually happening and that it was nothing new.

The fork with his chocolate cake was almost in her mouth when Mickey turned toward her, his eyebrow raised.

Her hand froze. Her eyes widened. She turned the fork around and held it out to him. Mickey leaned forward and took the bite.

"That's good cake." He rolled his eyes and said in a husky voice, "That's the best chocolate cake I have ever had."

Parker looked annoyed. He picked up his fork, cut off another bite of cake and held it up. He leaned toward her and then slid the fork into his mouth. "Yeah, the best I've ever had."

Toby laughed then turned to join a conversation between Marcus and LeShawn.

Mickey took another bit of cake on his fork and, leaning toward Parker, quietly said, "Open up, baby."

Parker looked into his eyes, her nostrils flared, and she opened her mouth. He slid his fork into her mouth. She closed her teeth and lips on the fork. Mickey slowly pulled it out of her mouth, watching her eyes. He cut off another piece of cake and held it out to her.

"I can feed myself," she whispered.

"Where's the fun in that."

She took the fork from his hand and with raised eyebrows looked over his shoulder.

Mickey turned and found all eyes on them.

"So, what's next?" he asked, ignoring the sudden awkward vibe in the room. "Which club are we going to?"

LeShawn answered. "You pick the club, Money. This is your turf. We haven't lived here for like ten years."

"Okay, pamper it is."

They finished their coffees; Parker finished the

chocolate cake and most of the lemon chiffon. Mickey signed the tab for the meal before they left the club and piled into limos to go to Pamper.

The line to get into Pamper was around the block. The limo dropped them off at the door. Mickey approached the doorman and held out a folded $50.

"Mr. Finn, nice to see you again," the doorman said as he took the folded bill and pulled open the door.

Mickey stood back while the band preceded him into the club. He heard the chatter going down the line:

"Is that Temptation?"

"Oh my God, LeShawn Rollins—I love him."

"It is them."

"I don't care how long we have to wait, we are getting in, girlfriend!"

Parker was last in line. The doorman put an arm out to stop her. He looked at Parker, then to Mickey. "You know there is a dress code, Mr. Finn. This is too casual."

"What's the problem, man," Parker demanded.

"Too casual," the doorman responded.

Parker looked down the line of people waiting to get in. "Jeans seem to be acceptable," she said.

"They are," the doorman responded.

"So what? The T-shirt? Is that it?"

"Yes, too casual, ma'am."

"Fuck me," Parker said as she pulled her T-shirt out of her shorts and over her head. She wore a red lace demi bra that cupped her perfect tits. One quick move, though, and a nipple might be peeking out. "How's this?"

"That'll get you in," the doorman said with a smirk.

Mickey growled and shot him a look as he put his hand on Parker's lower back. His hand tingled at contact with her smooth skin.

Parker shoved her T-shirt at the doorman and stalked into the club followed by Mickey.

"Sorry about that, Parker," Mickey said.

"No problem, Rod. I was willing to lose the shorts too."

Mickey gulped. "Glad you didn't have to."

"C'mon, Rod, get me drunk." She preceded him into the club, his hand on her lower back.

They met the guys at the bar. He ordered shots of tequila. They were being noticed. Word spread through the club and before long they were being mobbed by women, fans, and some old friends from when they lived there.

Parker was being crowded up against Mickey's body. She pushed her body backward, trying to force the crush back and make some room for herself. Mickey put his hands on her waist, picked her up, and plunked her ass on the bar.

"Better," he asked.

Another round of shots appeared in front of them. He handed one to Parker, clinked her glass and downed it.

"She can't be up there," the bartender said as he poured another round of shots.

"I'm being crushed," she retorted.

"Not my problem," the bartender said. "It's the law."

"Okay, then," Parker said as she took another shot and slammed her glass on the bar. She turned toward Mickey, put her hands in his hair and pulled him in for a kiss. She caught him by surprise but went with what he thought would be a casual kiss. Parker slid her hands out of his hair, down to his shoulders and around his neck.

He wasn't prepared for her kiss. His body tensed when her lips touched his, but it didn't take long for him to relax and take control of the kiss. He slid her down the bar and lifted her against him, one hand on her ass the other on her back. He turned to lean against the bar.

She pressed her breasts into his chest, her arms wrapped around his neck. Someone bumped into them, pushing Mickey to the side. He pulled away from the kiss, looking into Parker's eyes. Heat flowed between them. They both seemed to realize where they were. Mickey took his hand off her ass. She dropped her legs and slid down his body.

She leaned against him for a moment, then looked up at him with a wide smile on her face, "Wow, Rod, you are so hot," she said.

Mickey threw his head back and laughed. He turned, picked up two more shot glasses, gave her one and together they downed their drinks.

The music was blaring and they were still being crowded against the bar. Mickey put his hand on Parker's shoulder and pushed her through the crowd to an area with less people.

One of the bouncers came up to him. "We have a VIP section," he yelled into Mickey's ear, "you and your friends might want to sit there." He pointed to stairs leading to a mezzanine level overlooking the bar and dance floor.

Mickey nodded his head. He took Parker's hand in his and led her up the stairs into the VIP section. The bouncer approached the other guys, pointing out the VIP section. They all ended up there, eventually closing down the club, dancing, laughing, talking, and drinking.

Mickey stole glances at Parker all night long. She didn't approach him again although their eyes met time and again, but he couldn't get that kiss out of his mind. The last thing he remembered was downing another shot with Toby.

CHAPTER 3
Mickey

His phone was ringing. No! Mickey rolled over onto his back. It took him a moment to confirm that yes, he was in his own bed. Yes, he was naked. Yes, he was alone. Yes, his phone was ringing. Yes, his head hurt.

Mickey picked up his phone and held it up to his ear without speaking.

"Bro," Toby said. "You feel me?"

Mickey groaned.

"We're leaving at six tonight. It's only noon. I'm coming over. I want to spend a couple more hours with you."

"How are you even talking?"

"You are out of drinking practice, man. It's the rockstar life. Take a shower, down some Tylenol. I should be there in an hourish."

$$$

He felt a bit more human an hour later when his doorbell rang. He opened the door and Toby strolled in. He was about to close the door when he noticed Parker on the top step.

"Toby said I could come," she explained.

"Of course. Come in, baby." Mickey held the door open for her. She entered the foyer and he closed the door.

She turned toward him. She lifted her hand and laid it on his cheek. He bent down toward her. She put her other hand on his other cheek and leaned her forehead against his. "You look a little rough, Rod. Are you okay?"

"I'm better now." He smiled at her.

She brushed her lips lightly against his.

Mickey groaned. He wanted more, something like that kiss last night. Yeah, that would be good.

"Mickey?" Toby called from inside his house.

He met Parker's eyes before responding. "Coming."

Mickey was standing at the island with a coffee in his hand. Toby was seated on the other side. What they were talking about, Mickey couldn't say. He was watching Parker. She was walking around looking at his house. She looked at the art on the wall, the accessories on the furniture, she trailed her fingers over the fabric of his sofa. At last, she stopped in front of a wall covered with books, photos, and various items he had picked up on his travels.

Toby's cell rang. He looked at the display and answered it, turning away from Mickey. Mickey went to stand beside Parker.

"You read?" he asked her.

"Since I was six. I'm better at it now though," she responded.

"What do you read?"

"Who's this?" She picked up a framed photo, pulling it closer to her so she could take in every detail.

He watched her eyes examine the photo. He took a step closer to her. Fuck, he wanted to touch her. "That's me and Toby when we were kids."

She looked at him, studying his face for a moment and then looked at the picture again. She smiled. "You were cute." She put the picture back. She ran her fingers down the spines of the books on the shelf in front of her. "Have you read any of these?"

"Some of them."

"What are you reading now?"

"I hate to admit it, but I'm reading romance," she said. "Nowadays, it's like erotica. Pure escapism. You should read some. Maybe pick up a few tips."

"Tips on what?"

"You know, tongue usage, cock placement, nipple manipulation."

"Maybe I wrote those." He teased her, a grin on his face.

She met his eyes, she was breathless when she said, "Really?"

He shrugged his shoulders. "Maybe."

"Let's go for lunch," Toby said from behind them.

Man, he loved his brother. But at this moment, Mickey wished he were anywhere else.

"What do you prefer? Eat in? Go out?" Mickey asked.

"Hey, do they still sell those chilli cheeseburgers at Max's?"

"Sure do. Is that what you want?"

"I think that's exactly what we could all use at this moment," Toby said. "Nothing like some hot, spicy, greasy burgers after a night of drinking."

Mickey chuckled. "Sounds great, Toby. Let's go."

CHAPTER 4
Mickey

Lately, this was Mickey's favorite time of day. It was late, he was sitting in his office, the lights turned off, with two fingers of whiskey in the glass in his hand, looking down at the city, lit up and beautiful. He cleared his mind so he could spend a few minutes remembering those beautiful brown eyes, that tone of sarcasm in her words, the way she reacted to him, almost against her will. He had never had that type of electricity with any other woman. It was interesting, exciting.

Temptation had left the city six weeks ago. He stayed in touch with his brother via text but he hadn't heard from Parker, nor did he expect to. They had not exchanged numbers. He was surprised how thoughts of her managed to stay with him after all this time though. If this kept up, he would make an effort to find her, get in touch.

He didn't have much time for a relationship. He was always busy. After he had closed that deal with Benson, he had started the wheels turning on the development. He knew what he wanted to do with the property but now he had to get the plans and specs drawn up. He had to apply for permits, obtain financing…the to-do list was long.

That was just his new project. He had a number of others on the go, too—construction underway on several projects; other buildings nearing completion and headed for lease up; shopping centres with tenants moving in; a million small details to be tended to. It's not that he had his finger on the pulse of every project—that's what he had employees for, and damn good ones—but even they needed to meet with him to deal with problems that arose.

Would it be nice to have someone in his life? Sure, but where would they fit in? He worked long hours. He got to the office every morning by seven. He usually worked until six and later. After the office, he still had obligations, the occasional event, community meetings, and neighborhood committees wanting a say in his proposed developments, drinks with friends.

In the last interview he had given, the interviewer had asked him when enough was enough. He was a billionaire, he had enough money to last a lifetime, didn't he want to take time to enjoy the fruits of his labor, maybe ease back a bit? That was not the first time he had been asked that particular question or a variation of it. He had employees relying on him, young people starting families, buying their first home, established people with children to put through university, older people wanting to retire with some financial security. He couldn't just end it all, cut all those people loose and leave them adrift, maybe ruin them. So, enough was never enough.

He savored the last sip of whiskey, put his glass down,

and leaned back in his chair, closing his eyes. Parker was waiting for him, in his house, in her bikini. Toby did not make an appearance in this scenario. He picked her up and sat her on his kitchen island, standing between her legs. He twisted one of his hands in her hair, pulling her lips to his. With his other hand he undid the knot of her bikini top at her neck. She leaned forward, her bikini bra falling down. He took her lips in a savage kiss. His other hand now testing the fullness of her breast before playing with her nipple. She moaned against his lips, scooting her ass over the island, closer to the erection straining his jeans.

His phone rang. "Fuck," he swore as he adjusted his cock before picking it up.

"Hey, bro," Toby greeted him. What was it with Toby these days? He was constantly interrupting at the wrong time.

"Toby," he ground out.

"You okay, Mickey? You sound strange."

"Yeah, I'm okay. I've just got a frog in my throat." *And a log in my pants*, he thought before he coughed into the phone. He wasn't about to admit he'd been about to get off thinking about his brother's drummer.

"Hey, Silvio's back, so we're sending Parker home. She's got a layover in town for a couple days. Do you think you can pick her up at the airport tomorrow night at seven? Maybe let her stay at your place for the next day or so before her flight out?"

Now Mickey was glad he had picked up the phone. "Umm, sure. That's strange that she has a layover here. Did she want to visit in the city?"

"Well, she didn't say she didn't want to visit. Let's just say I got your back, bro."

"What does that mean?"

"You both seemed to vibe, so I thought, why not?"

"Toby…"

"No problem, bro, if you don't want to, just say so. I can book a hotel for her. She can always cash in her ticket and arrange a flight out. What do you say?"

"Okay. Seven tomorrow night at the airport, but only if it's okay with her."

"She'll be there at seven. She might not stay but she will be there at seven. Thanks, bro, I owe you for this."

"You have no idea, Toby. How's the tour?"

Half an hour later, they disconnected. Mickey smiled. Tomorrow night at seven could not come fast enough.

CHAPTER 5
Parker

Fucking Toby Finn. What, was he pimping her out to his brother now? Fucking Toby Finn. Fucking Mickey Finn.

Parker exited the airport, pulling her suitcase behind her. She was wearing a pair of high-waisted navy slacks and a white bandeau top under a military style navy blazer with gold buttons, gold braid detail, and gold epaulets. She wore a black fedora pulled over her eyes and black stiletto boots. She knew she looked good. She felt good and she needed all the ammunition she had when facing Fucking Mickey Finn.

First of all, he had taken her breath away when she had opened her eyes to that mountain of a man in the green room at the arena. She knew he wasn't a stripper. That was a joke. If there was a stripper for the band it would have been a woman, definitely not a man. She wanted to be all over that mass of man and couldn't help herself from running her hands over his chest. Yeah, and he liked it. She had felt his muscles shudder. God knows what she would have done if he had let her slide her hand into his pants.

Kissing him had been a tease that had backfired on her. Yummy.

When she joined the rest of the band before hitting the stage, she had asked who the fuck that guy was. Of course, it was Toby's big brother. For the past week the guys had been talking about "Money", she thought maybe it was their old weed dealer or something. Boy, had she been wrong.

That whole night with him kept replaying in her mind. How he stood in front of the bathroom door while she was in there. She'd lost count of the number of times someone had walked in on her naked or partially clothed because there was no lock on the door. Then that little episode with Melanie, her fan. He didn't like her talking to that roadie for so long. But what she kept coming back to was at his club when he had fed her that chocolate cake. He had whispered "open up, baby" with that sexy deep voice while looking in her eyes. She had made herself come a couple of times recalling that. Oh yeah.

And at the bar, pushed up against him, well, maybe she wasn't that crowded, but it turned out okay, right? She had wanted to kiss him since the arena and, his lips had delivered everything she had hoped they would.

She avoided him in the VIP section for the rest of the night because, hand to God, she would have fucked him right there in front of everyone. There was something between them, they could both feel it, but, first, she was leaving never to see him again and, second, he was Toby's brother. Like that would not have been awkward for the rest of the tour.

Then the next day at his house. He had called her baby

again. He was going to kiss her in the foyer, if it hadn't been for Toby. Fucking Toby Finn. When Mickey spoke to her in front of the bookcase, he had taken a step closer to her, she had not backed away. She could feel a pull toward him, the heat from his body. Then when he had hinted that perhaps he had written some of those erotic scenes in the books she read, well, her panties were instantly wet when he said that, looking at her with those eyes and that sexy voice. Fucking Mickey Finn.

The man was dangerous. That was the problem. He was not a sharer; he was a keeper. She was a free spirit, she was young, she was attractive, she worked with some of the sexiest men in the music world, fun shit happened. He would expect her to stop that. He would want to keep her to himself, no sharsies.

She knew he was interested in her. She could see it in his eyes, feel it in the way he treated her. She felt he was the type of man who would do whatever it took to get what he wanted. If he wanted her, would she be able to fight against him? She wasn't sure. She wasn't sure she would want to. Fucking Mickey Finn!

So now she was here. Fucking Toby Finn couldn't arrange a direct flight to L.A. Not only that, there was a two-day layover, but, lucky her, Fucking Mickey Finn was going to pick her up at the airport and put her up for the day and a half before her flight to L.A. Fucking Toby Finn was one of her favorite people right now.

"Parker," someone called her name.

She looked across the street and saw Mickey, his hand in the air. He was dressed in a dark suit, a button-down shirt with the top button undone, no tie. She couldn't help herself. She smiled at him. He jogged across the road to her. He seemed to be running in slow motion. She shook her head and then he was standing in front of her. He hugged her, took the handle to her suitcase in one hand and her hand in his other, pulling her across the road, after him.

"The car's over here," he said.

Parker had to jog to keep up with him, her heart soaring. Fucking Mickey Finn!

He had a driver! The driver stowed her suitcase in the trunk. Mickey held the door open for her while she got in the car. He closed the door and walked to the other side of the car before getting in. He spoke to the driver before climbing in. The car started, they eased into traffic and they left the airport.

He turned to her. "You hungry? Do you want something to eat before we go home?"

"I just want to find a bed," she said. "I haven't really slept in like thirty-six hours."

Mickey called to his driver, "Tony, take us home." He turned to her. "How was your flight?"

"Long," she responded, looking out the window. She could feel him looking at her. She wasn't going to look at him. She was only here for a couple of days. She was not sure whether starting something with him was a good idea. Maybe tomorrow before she left, a quickie to take the edge of him off her mind.

She sighed heavily. She felt as if she was sinking into the soft leather of the car seats. "I'm really tired." She yawned. She put her hand out to him.

Mickey took her hand in his. He lifted it to his lips and kissed her palm. "I've got you, baby," he said as he pulled her into his side. She rested her head on his shoulder. He was so solid and warm. She closed her eyes, inhaling his scent. He smelled comfortable, like suede and pine trees on a wet day.

"You smell nice," she said quietly.

She felt his laugh rumble in his chest.

$$$

She was wrapped in a fuzzy warm cloud. She snuggled deeper into the softness enveloping her body. No matter how much she wanted to go back to sleep, nature was calling. She opened her eyes. She was alone in a strange room. Warm sunlight was streaming through the blinds on the window. There was an open door to the side of her room, an en suite.

After taking care of business, it occurred to her that she was only wearing her panties and a large T-shirt that fell to mid-thigh. Her bandeau top was down around her waist. She wriggled out of the bandeau, throwing it on the bed and left the room. She smelled coffee and followed her nose to the end of the hallway.

She found herself in Mickey's living area looking at the familiar bookcase. She turned toward the kitchen and stopped. Mickey was on the other side of the island, shirtless. He was reading the paper, raising a cup of coffee to his lips when he looked up and saw her.

"Good morning. There's coffee," he said.

She couldn't help herself. She examined every inch of his bare torso and muscular arms. His hair was damp, most of it pushed back onto his skull with drier strands falling down onto his forehead. She would like to run her hands over his body and into his hair. She smirked. She liked what she was looking at.

She felt him watching her as she ogled him. When her eyes finally met his, he raised his eyebrows. She didn't look away or blush. She tilted her head in his direction with a challenge. Yeah, she liked what she was looking at. What are you going to do about it?

She walked to the coffee pot and poured a cup. "Do you have any cream or milk?"

"In the fridge."

The fridge was directly behind him. She pulled the door open, took out the cream, poured some in her coffee, put back the cream and closed the door. She turned and leaned against the fridge, ogling the back half of that body. He was wearing a pair of sweats, hanging low on his hips. He had a great ass. His back was defined and muscular. She leaned forward to get a whiff of him. He smelled clean, citrusy.

"Everything okay back there?" he asked glancing over his shoulder.

"Do you always have coffee in the morning half-naked?"

"No. Sometimes I'm completely naked. But you're here, so I thought I would put on some pants."

"Too bad."

He chuckled.

She walked around the island and picked up a section of the paper that he was not reading.

"A newspaper, how retro," she said.

"I spend too much time on digital devices. I like the smell and feel of a paper," he told her.

She briefly skimmed the section she held. Just below the fold, the italics in the bottom of a box caught her attention:

Billionaire Mickey Finn picking up an exotic beauty at the airport

What the…she flipped the paper over. There was a large picture of Mickey holding her hand at the airport and pulling her along after him. He was looking down at her smiling. She was looking up at him.

"Did you see this?" she demanded.

"Yes."

"So, you're a billionaire?"

He didn't answer the question.

"You have a billion dollars?"

"Not on me right now."

"More than a billion?"

"Maybe." He seemed a little annoyed.

A billion dollars! That sum was almost incomprehensible! As for the picture in the paper, she was surprised to see herself there. It was not as if she hadn't made the papers before on the arm of one famous musician or the other. It didn't bother her. They didn't seem to know who she was though and that bothered her even less.

"By the way, Mr. Finn," she said sternly, capturing his attention, "did you happen to see what happened to my clothes? Cuz I seem to recall wearing more than my underwear and I don't know where this T-shirt came from."

"I wanted you to be comfortable, Parker. I have seen you in a bikini, this was no different," he said in a tone of voice that implied the logic of that statement. "That's one of my T-shirts. I didn't want to go through your suitcase. That would have been creepy, don't you think?"

"I do think. Thanks."

"Let me know if you need help getting dressed later. I'll make time to assist you."

"Thanks for the offer, Rod. Back at you, by the way."

They smiled at each other over their coffee cups. A ringtone broke the mood. It took a moment for Parker to realize it was her phone.

"My purse! Where's my purse?"

"On the side table," he pointed.

She ran to the table and pulled out her phone, answering the call.

"Hello. Brynn? What's up? Yeah, I'm here, just for a bit. I'm leaving tomorrow. Yes, Mickey Finn. Yeah. I know, right!"

She looked at him, then looked away, walking toward the windows making up the living room wall.

"What? How did you get involved in that? Oh, that's so nice. Really? Yeah, I would do that. How long do you think? A couple weeks? Where is the studio? Yeah, I'll do it pro bono. Don't tell anyone though, I'm going to have every agent begging me for pro bono work. So, I'll see you on Monday then at ten? Can't wait."

She ended the call and turned back to the island. She

was looking down at her phone, scrolling through screens. She looked up at Mickey. He was watching her.

"Do you know Brynn Williams?" she asked.

"I don't believe I do. Should I?"

"Yeah, well, she's a producer I work with. She's in town right now." Parker was still scrolling on her phone. She stopped to read something.

"And," Mickey prompted her.

"Yeah, so she just asked me to work on an album with her so I'm going to be here longer than just a couple days, probably a couple weeks." She looked up at him. "I'm going to get a room downtown at the Fairmont." She held her phone out to Mickey to show him the listing she had found. "Do you know it?"

"Yes. It's one of the best hotels in the city," he said. "I've been there a few times for functions and dinner, never overnight."

"Well, I thought I might as well just go now." Mickey was watching her, his expression unreadable. "Do you think you or Tony could give me a lift there. I can't ask you to put me up for another month."

"You don't have to ask. You can stay here. I insist you stay here, Parker. There is nothing to discuss," he said. He was such a boss man.

But she wanted to have some fun. "I really can't inconvenience you like that, Mickey. That's like a whole other month."

"Like I said, Parker, it's no problem. You'll stay here." His tone of voice discouraged further discussion.

So what? "But the studio is downtown and that's not

very close, right. If I got a room at the Fairmont I could just walk to the studio. I don't know how to get there from your house."

He actually sighed. "Tony will drive you and pick you up. You have your own room and bathroom here." There was a finality to that statement.

"I'm sure Tony has better things to do than drive me around, Mickey."

He put down the paper, walked around the island and stood in front of her, forcing her to tilt her head back to look up at him. "I pay him to drive places. It is no problem for him to drive you to the studio and pick you up. It's his job."

She crossed her arms in front of her and looked down. "I..."

His hand was on her face. His thumb drew a little circle on her cheek before going to the corner of her mouth. "You'll stay here."

Oh my goodness! He was standing right in front of her with his bare chest in her face, touching her and looking at her with those eyes and speaking to her in that voice! She knew what his lips felt like. Was she starting to get wet? Yikes.

She turned her head and parted her lips, sucking his thumb into her mouth. He watched her through hooded eyes. She pulled her head back, sliding his thumb out. She met his eyes and then sucked his thumb back into her mouth, watching him. She didn't have to look down to know his cock was tenting his sweatpants. Desire was in his eyes and written on his face.

She pulled her head back again, sliding his thumb out of her mouth. "So, it's settled then. I guess I'll stay here. Thanks, Mickey. Where did I put my coffee?" She stepped around him and went to lean against the island with both hands holding her coffee cup. She was looking down, reading an article in the paper when a heavy hand slapped her backside.

"What the fuck! What was that for?"

"Oh, you know what that was for, you tease. I don't appreciate that type of thing unless you're going to follow up. Just remember that next time you feel like playing with me, baby."

She put her coffee cup down and rubbed her backside where he'd spanked her. She'd never been called on her bullshit before. It was kind of hot. She met his eyes, reassessing him and realizing that he was a lot more dangerous to her than she had initially thought.

CHAPTER 6
Mickey

Maybe it wasn't such a good idea for him to have insisted she stay at his place. They were both dancing around the attraction that was between them. He was interested in her, she knew it, and that was something she seemed to be willing to use to her advantage.

It wasn't about his money though. She was quite wealthy herself. He had Googled her after he met her. She was from a wealthy family. An only child. A musical genius who could play piano, violin, anything, but drums and percussion instruments were what she chose. She had graduated from Julliard, had been courted by symphony orchestras from around the world and had even played for Boston for a few months before giving it up and becoming a studio musician.

She was well known and well paid for her time. She had played on some of the most popular albums for the biggest names in the music industry. As a studio musician she had a certain level of anonymity but she was linked with some of the hottest musicians in the industry and not just for her musical talent.

Mickey felt her interest in him, he would have to be blind to not be able to read her thoughts as she scanned his body. But she was almost blasé about it, seeming to ignore him at times and argumentative with him at others. He couldn't quite get a read on her though. Was her interest in him purely physical or was she interested in something more? Time would tell and he had just managed to buy himself some more time with her.

Right now, they were walking through a farmers' market. He was following her from kiosk to kiosk in her cut-off jeans, fraying at the edges, the pockets peeking out in the front, her ass cheeks just barely covered in the back. She wore a bikini top covered by a sweater that ended just below her bust.

"Umm, smell this," she said as she held a melon up to his nose. "This is just right. Do you like honeydew?"

"I do." He smiled down at her.

She bought the melon, put it in a mesh bag and handed the bag to him. She took his hand in hers as they continued down the aisle.

They bought more fruit and some vegetables. She also bought some scented candles, some homemade soap, and body lotion made from goat's milk. They came to the end of one aisle and turned to go up the next aisle and then back to the car. She came to a sudden halt, she groaned and turned into him, pushing her face into his chest.

"What is it, baby?" he asked, concerned.

"Oh my God, Mickey,"

"What?"

She looked up at him, turned so that her back was pushed up against him and pointed. "That!"

He followed the path of her pointed finger and laughed. A table covered with mini cakes, chocolate, vanilla, cheesecake, pies, muffins, cookies, and slices.

"Parker, you can handle this. I know you can," he teased her gently. He pushed her forward with his body, angling toward the table.

"I don't know, Mickey. I don't know if this is a good idea,"

"I'm with you, baby. I'll take care of you."

They stood in front of the table.

"Hi," the baker greeted them. "All homemade with fresh ingredients. See anything you like?"

"Ah, yeah," Parker stuttered. She looked up at Mickey. "Help?"

"We'll take two of the cheesecakes, one chocolate cake, and one of the hummingbird cakes," he ordered. "Is that good, baby?"

"Yes, that's great."

They waited while the baker packed the cakes. Parker leaned her body against his looking up at him. "I'm going to make dinner tonight," she said.

He looked down at her and smiled. "Just for buying you cake?"

"Yeah, and bringing me here and letting me stay at your place. This has been a really nice day, Mickey. Thank you."

"I'm enjoying the day too," he said.

He leaned forward to take the cake box from the baker. Parker pushed against him and kissed his cheek. He turned toward her and she brushed her lips against his. With a lopsided grin she continued down the aisle, holding his hand.

$$$

Vegetables were roasting in the oven, pots were bubbling, pans were frying, the aroma in the house was tantalizing. Parker flitted around the kitchen while Mickey sat at the island working on his laptop.

"Supper in twenty or so," Parker said. "You going to put that away?" She pointed a wooden spoon at his laptop.

"Yes, ma'am." He smiled as he shut down and closed the laptop. He picked it up and took it into his office.

He came back to the kitchen, set two places on the island, then brought down a bottle of red wine. He got two wine glasses and poured. He picked up one glass and held it out to Parker. She took a quick sip, put it down and turned the steaks sizzling in the pan.

Five minutes later she was plating the meal and placing the dishes on the island. Mickey waited for her to join him before he cut into his steak and brought it to his mouth. He chewed his steak, the juices running down his throat.

"Wow, this is delicious, baby. Where did you learn to cook like this?"

"My dad," she said simply.

"Your dad? Not your mom?"

"No, my dad. You know he owns a national chain of steakhouses, right?" She glanced briefly at him as he nodded his head. "Well, he was the cook in the original restaurant.

He wanted me to be self-sufficient, my mom wanted me to marry rich and be a princess. Dad won."

"And what did your mom teach you?"

"Oh, you know, makeup, hair, clothes, manipulation. All the necessities."

"Manipulation? I didn't know that was a standard skill to be passed down to princesses."

"For my mom, it was. She was an excellent teacher."

"What kind of manipulation?"

Parker shrugged her shoulders. She finished her meal and stood. He took the last bite of steak and put down his utensils. She leaned over and picked up his plate. She went around the island and put the dishes in the sink. She came back to him. He swiveled his chair toward her.

She put her hands on his thighs, he opened his legs enough for her to get closer to him, leaning against his chest. She leaned her head against him, drawing circles on his chest with her finger. He put his arm around her back. She looked up at him, raising her chin, he leaned forward, his lips almost on hers.

"Do you want dessert?" she asked breathlessly.

"What are you offering?" he asked as he lightly kissed her cheek.

"Cake."

"Cake?"

"Yeah. Do you want some…coffee with that cake?" she whispered into his mouth.

Mickey groaned.

"See, Rod, Manipulation 101," she said as she turned

and walked to the fridge to plate the cakes they had bought that afternoon.

She came back to him and placed his cake in front of him. She moved to go around him to her chair. He grabbed her wrist. He took the other plate out of her hand and placed it on the island in front of her chair. He took her other wrist and pulled her in between his legs.

"What did I tell you this morning, baby? About teasing me?" His mouth was at her ear, asking her in a strained voice.

"You said, don't do it," she replied.

"And if you did? What was going to happen?"

"You were going to…" She couldn't say the words. His hand was trailing down her back, stopping on her ass. "Don't do it, please," she pleaded.

"Why not? Did you tease me?"

"Yes," she whined.

He gently tapped her behind. "Do you deserve it?"

She was leaning against him. "Yes. No. Yes." She rubbed her thighs together.

"What is it, baby? Yes, or no? Do you deserve it?" His voice was husky and low in her ear.

"No, I don't," she said. She was bouncing on the balls of her feet, nervous and so hot right now with his hand on her ass.

"Why not?"

"Cuz this," she looked up into his eyes. She put her hands in his hair and pulled his head down to hers. She attacked his mouth and he responded, quickly taking control of the kiss. He wrapped both his arms around her and lifted her to straddle his thighs. She arched her back, pushing her breasts into his chest.

His tongue teased her lips, making her open her mouth to allow his tongue entrance. She molded herself to him, wrapping her arms around his neck. It was as if she couldn't get close enough to him. He held her, one hand on her ass, the other on her back. She was eager and responsive to his kisses.

His cock strained against his pants, wanting to join the party, pushing into her crotch. She moaned into his mouth and then put a hand on his chest pushing away from him. It took him a moment to process her actions. He pulled away from her, loosening his grip.

"I didn't mean to get so carried away," she said, looking away from him. "I'm sorry." She pushed away from him, sliding off his thighs to stand on the floor.

He was hard from wanting her. This is not how he thought this was going to end. He ran his hand through his hair and stood. He couldn't be angry at her. He hadn't meant to get so lost in that kiss either. There was just something about her that made him lose control.

He stood. "I've got work to do anyway," he said, looking down at her.

She refused to meet his eyes. He caught her chin and forced her to look at him. "It's okay, baby."

A look of relief washed over her face. She grinned at him. "I'll put the cakes back in the fridge then. For later."

"Sure," he said as he left the kitchen. Moments later, the door to his office closed.

CHAPTER 7
Parker

Oh my God! She had never been kissed like that before. It was so easy to get lost in the emotions he brought up in her. He was lust and passion and heat. Maybe he *had* written some of those passages in the books she read. Holy mother…

She had to stop when she did or she would have been naked and begging for him within the next five minutes. She was still wet, still wanting, but she forced herself to clean the kitchen and put the cakes back in the fridge before going to her room. She closed the door, flung herself on her bed, pulled out her vibrator and came to images of him leaning over her pounding mercilessly into her pussy.

She ended her day by taking a shower and reading until she was too tired to keep her eyes open.

$$$

Sunday started much the same way. She came into the living area to find Mickey at the island reading the paper, half-dressed, drinking a cup of coffee.

She stumbled to the pot, poured a cup and went to the fridge for cream. She leaned against the fridge door, looking at his perfection. He glanced over his shoulder at her.

"Still wearing pants, Rod?" She didn't hide her examination of him, holding her cup up to her mouth, her eyes devouring him.

He swivelled his chair around, facing her. His eyes took in her sleep-tousled hair, her half-opened eyes, and slid down her body. He paused at her breasts; she liked the way his T-shirt pulled across her fullness. As he looked, her nipples tightened. His eyes briefly shot to hers and returned to her breasts, smiling. She knew her nipples were peaking under the thin cotton of the T-shirt and why wouldn't they with him looking at her like that?

He tore his eyes away from her breasts and continued downward, stopping where the junction of her thighs were under his large T-shirt. He stopped, looked into her eyes again, almost as if he could see the wetness there, before returning and skimming down her legs.

Parker smirked at him, pushed away from the fridge and walked around the island. She picked up the lifestyle section of the paper. She briefly skimmed the front page before going to the second page to the gossip column. On the second page there were pictures of her and Mickey at the farmers' market. She was holding up the melon to him in one picture and them kissing in the next picture. The caption read *Mickey Finn and his mystery woman at the farmers' market.*

"Did you see this?" she asked.

"No. What?"

He put down the business section and took the section she held out to him. He looked at the pictures and skimmed the column before handing it back to her. He looked at her. "And?"

"Are there photographers following you everywhere?"

"Not always. Are you upset?"

"No. Aren't you? They didn't mention your billions of dollars."

He laughed at her. "No, they didn't, but they did mention your exotic beauty. You make me look good."

"You hardly need me to make you look good."

"You find me attractive, baby?"

"You know I do, Rod. Even with your clothes on."

"If you want them off, just say the word, Parker."

"Don't hold your breath."

He grinned at her. "I've got some things to do today. I'm going to be out most of the day. Where's your phone?"

"What do you need my phone for?"

"I want to give you some numbers, just in case."

She pulled up the hem of the T-shirt and grabbed her phone out of the back pocket of her shorts and handed it to him.

He took it from her and opened the contacts. "This is Tony's number. If you need a ride somewhere, just call him," he said as he entered the information. "This is my number if you need to get in touch with me for whatever reason you can call or text." He entered his number. Seconds later his phone rang. "And now I have your number," he said as he handed her phone back to her. "Are you going to be all right here alone?"

"Yes, daddy, I'll be fine," she said, rolling her eyes.

He grabbed her chin and made her look up at him. "I may be a lot of things, Parker, but I am not your daddy."

She could tell he was annoyed at her for that. He continued to stare at her. She didn't know what he expected her to say or do. She crossed her eyes and stuck her tongue out at him before jerking her chin out of his grasp.

"I'll be fine. I need to practice anyway."

"Okay then. You have my number, and Tony's if you need anything."

$$$

The house was so quiet when he was gone. She did some stretches, a few yoga poses, and then put her buds in her ears. She tuned into her practice music. She rolled her neck, then her shoulders, and began to move her sticks. It wasn't long before she was in the zone. Eyes closed, nothing but the music existed for her, her hands keeping time with the beat, shooting out to hit the high hat or the cymbal that were not there.

Hours later she put down her sticks and pulled the buds out of her ears. She stood and stretched again. She began to explore the house. She walked down the hall where her bedroom was. There were other doors there. She opened them and found two more guestrooms with en suites.

At the end of the hall, she opened the door to Mickey's master bedroom. The room was huge and centered in the room was a massive bed. There was a couch and chairs forming a conversation area at the far end. On the other end there was a door that led into his spacious closet. Parker ran her hands over the shirts and suits neatly hanging in color-coordinated sections. There was an island in the middle of room. The drawers, she guessed, contained his underwear and socks, maybe some jewelry. She didn't look. On a tray on top of the island sat bottles of cologne. She picked them up, one by one, smelling them, until she found her favorite one.

After the closet was the en suite. It was all marble with a huge tub and a walk-in shower. She sat in the tub and then slid down the backrest until she was laying full-out in the tub. *This would be nice for a bubble bath*, she thought, *or sex*.

Heading back out she was tempted to jump on his bed but didn't want to take the chance that he would know she had been in here. She closed the door, returned to the living room and explored the other half of the house. Another hallway.

She opened the first door and found a fully-equipped gym. That explained his appearance in the morning. He must work out first, shower, and then read the paper with a coffee. The next door was his office. His desk was clean with his closed laptop sitting in the centre. She walked around his desk and sat in his chair. She swivelled around in circles a few times. In front of his desk were two chairs. A round table with two more chairs was placed in the corner. A small TV was mounted on the wall across from his desk.

There was only one other door at the end of this hallway. She opened it and gasped. It was a full-sized pool! Except for the wall where the entrance was located. the rest of the room was floor-to-ceiling glass. The yard beyond was lushly landscaped with shrubs and trees. The pool room was completely hidden from neighboring houses and any prying eyes.

Parker shrieked with glee. She stripped off her clothes and jumped into the warm water.

CHAPTER 8
Mickey

Mickey didn't know what to expect when he came home but he didn't expect to find Parker missing. He saw evidence of her everywhere. Her drumsticks were on the living room table, her coffee cup on the island. He walked to her bedroom. Her door was open but she wasn't there.

He turned in the other direction. The gym? Maybe. No, not there. Not in his office but why would she be?

He went to the end of the hall and opened the door. His breath caught in his throat and he froze. Parker was on her back, floating in the pool with her eyes closed. She was naked. His eyes freely roamed her body, finally seeing what he had imagined beneath her clothes. Her breasts were just the right size to fit his palm. Her nipples a dusky brown. Her body was toned. His eyes travelled to her pussy. It was smooth, the lips puffy and inviting. His cock stood up, slyly suggesting that he join her in the pool.

The open door must have caused a cool breeze to circulate into the room. Parker's eyes popped open. She saw him standing in the doorway looking at her. "You didn't tell me you had a pool," she said.

Did she just push her breasts out of the water? "You didn't ask," he replied, nervously clearing his throat.

"Your house is incredible," she laughed as she spread her legs. "Why don't you join me, Rod?"

She was too much. There would be no winning for him in this situation. He swore, slamming the door behind himself as he headed into his office. He sat down, unzipped his pants and pulled out his throbbing cock. That girl was going to be the death of him. Was she purposefully playing with him? He stroked himself. Her tits would fit his hands perfectly, those nipples would peak nicely in his mouth. He stroked himself harder. That pussy! Yes, that pussy looked like it had been made for him, his mouth, his cock. He stroked himself faster. If she was here right now, she would be bent over this desk with her ass in the air and his cock pounding in and out of her wet pussy. His balls tightened. Yeah, she would be screaming his name, begging him to fuck her harder. One more stroke and he shot his load. He leaned back in his chair cursing his stupidity for insisting she stay at his house.

$$$

He had been in his office for hours. He'd jerked off twice more to images of her in the pool before he opened his laptop and set his mind to work. There was always something he needed to do: answer emails, review reports, draft correspondence. The hours flew by. By the time he shut down and closed his laptop it was dark outside and his stomach was asking for food.

He walked into the kitchen and opened the fridge, standing in the shaft of light, reviewing his options.

"I'm not sorry," a voice said behind him.

He looked over his shoulder. Parker stood there in a T-shirt and shorts. "Sorry for what?"

"For the pool. I'm not sorry I let you see me naked."

He blew out the breath he had been holding. "I'm not mad."

"You seemed pretty mad when you left."

"Well, I wasn't." He said it with finality, not wanting to pursue this line of conversation. He was glad when she let it drop. "I'm hungry," he stated. "How about you? Have you had supper?"

"No, not yet."

"Well then, let's do something about that. Do you want to go out? Order in? Make something? Your choice."

"Let's go out. Nowhere fancy though. I could go for some good diner food."

"Okay," he held out his hand to her, "let's go."

He drove them to Casey's Corner, a diner on the other side of town. They sat across from each other in a window booth. He had a meatloaf dinner with green beans and mashed potatoes. Parker had ordered chicken fingers and fries.

"So, tell me about your gig," he said.

"Brynn, the producer, grew up here," she told him. "A friend of hers from high school just opened a studio. He'd reached out to her a couple of months ago about a contest where she would produce a record for the winner. Just a promo for the studio."

"Sounds interesting." He encouraged her with a smile.

"Yeah, well, Brynn picked out three possible winners. The one she likes is a singer with a shit band so just getting some good back up would definitely improve the quality of whatever they put out. When Brynn saw that picture of you dragging me around the airport, she called me."

"Dragging you?"

"Yes," she looked into his eyes, laughing, "dragging me. You have long legs, Rod, I could barely keep up and I was exhausted. Here, try one of these, they're really good." She dipped a French fry in a pile of ketchup and held it up to his lips.

He reached out, took her hand and put the French fry in his mouth, chewing slowly. "They are good," he said, still holding her hand. Their eyes connected and held. He smiled at her as he rubbed a small circle on her hand with his thumb.

"You," she said breathlessly.

"Me?" he asked her, smirking.

"I think you know," she said as she pulled her hand out of his and picked up another French fry. She shuddered and looked at him again. "What did you do all day?"

"Not much, I went to some construction sites to check up on progress."

"What are you building?"

"Right now, I am preparing to break ground on a development in the Village," he said. "It's interesting. It's a large parcel where a hotel has been demolished. I also managed to get a few more blocks on the same side of the street so I'm tearing that down." He paused as he sipped his soda. "So, when that is all done, I'm going to redevelop the area into condos with commercial areas on the first two floors. There will be restaurants, offices, stores, that sort of thing."

"Wow. When will that be finished?"

"That is still a couple years away. In the meantime, I have a mall I'm offering for lease up on the south side of a city, in a new development, Potter's Creek."

"Help me with these fries. I saw cake on the menu, do you want dessert?"

"Do you?"

"I do, but I don't want to be the only one."

He had heard that line before. He picked up a fry. "What are the cake options?"

"They have a German chocolate torte. Those are always good. Do you want to share?"

"With you? Will you leave any for me?" he teased her.

She smiled, leaning over the table toward him. "You'd better be fast with your fork if you want any."

$$$

He was up and out of the house before Parker rolled out of bed. He began his day with a workout, a shower and then a cup of coffee with the paper. He pulled the sections apart, looking for the business section when her picture caught his eye.

They were on the front page of the lifestyle section again. They were in the diner. She was holding the French fry up to him and he was holding her hand. He raised his eyebrows at the headline:

Is the third time the charm? Billionaire Mickey Finn settling down?

He quickly scanned the article. Yeah, this was the third time they had been seen together, apparently two more times than he had ever been seen with any other woman. *Really?* he asked himself. Had he never dated anyone before? Sure, he must have. There was Maggie, no, that was more of a sex only thing behind closed doors. Paula, yeah, he had seen her a couple of times. Right? Noreen? No. Janice?

Fuck it. He had to go to work.

CHAPTER 9
Parker

Parker woke slowly. She loved this bed. She had never slept in anything like this. She was going to get one for herself when she went back home. She rolled over, starfishing—spreading her arms and legs. She thought about their fork fight over the cake last night and laughed.

Mickey Finn was such a man. Physically, he was a mountain, tall and defined. Emotionally though, yeah, he was all man. She thought about all the men she had had. Musicians. Most of them were emotional teenagers living their rock and roll dreams, never thinking past the next party, the next pussy, looking for a new something to excite them.

But Mr. Mickey Finn…she got a warm glow in her stomach when she thought of him and how he looked at her sometimes. He looked at her like he wanted to have her, to own her, body and soul. That was why he was so dangerous to her. She would like to give herself to him, her body anyway. She suspected he would lift her to new heights she had never experienced before.

Finally, she rolled out of bed and into the en suite. She

showered, running her hands over her naked body, imagining they were Mickey's hands caressing her breasts, twisting her nipples, claiming her pussy. She picked up her waterproof vibrator, yeah, she had thought ahead. She turned it on and held it up to her nipples, feeling them tighten, before putting the head to where it was really needed. She was already wet and waiting. She pushed it into her pussy hard. She leaned against the shower wall, the warm water beating down on her as she pinched her nipple with one hand and shoved her vibrator in and out of her aching pussy. She released her nipple and began to circle her clit. Yes, yes, yes. She screamed when she came.

She had a couple hours before she had to be at the studio. She had a coffee and was about to get dressed and practice a bit when a corner of the paper caught her eye. The word "billionaire" jumped out at her and it could only refer to Mickey. She pulled the paper free of the pile and saw their picture from the diner last night. She read the article with interest. Really, she thought. He had never dated anyone before it seemed. That was unbelievable. A man like him must have had a number of relationships.

No, it seems like he had had a revolving door of women on his arm but never more than once. Interesting. So, she assumed that he would be a one-time hit with her. Right now, they were dancing around each other, and she liked the dance, but there was no long term anything with Mickey Finn in her future. That was reassuring, she thought.

$$$

"Let's do it one more time, okay," Brynn said. She was in the control booth with the tech. Parker was drenched. They had been at this for hours, literally. The singer was good, the song had possibilities. It had great words and a catchy beat. The fucking band sucked though and that was why they were still here banging away at the same tune since this morning.

They were young, had been together for years, and were stubbornly loyal to each other. There had been a scene when Parker arrived at the studio…

She was ready to start working when she entered the control booth. She greeted Brynn and took off her coat. The band were standing around, not knowing what to do, waiting for instructions. One of them took a look at Parker in her bikini.

"I didn't know there would be entertainment. All fucking right, sweetheart."

Parker rolled her eyes, like she hadn't had that reaction before. She pulled her sticks out of her coat pocket and met the charmer's eyes with a steady gaze. She said nothing, just stared at him. He began to fidget.

Brynn laughed, breaking the awkward vibe that had sprung up. "This is Parker Chen. Maybe you've heard of her. The best drummer in the business right now. She'll be laying the tracks for this album."

The band exchanged confused looks. "But I'm the drummer," one of them said.

"Yeah, Zach's our drummer," another one added.

Parker sat down and waited for Brynn to clean up this mess.

"Listen, guys, Zach, you want the best rights? You want to

make the charts with your music? Well, I've gotta be honest with you, Zach isn't right for this album."

"What is that supposed to mean?" Zach sort of whined and yelled at the same time.

"What it means, Zach, is that you can't seem to keep a beat, and what that means is that everyone else is off and if everyone else is off then Pax is singing over the music instead of with it and it is a fucking mess that no one would want to listen to."

"But we won the contest. You picked us," Zach stated.

"I didn't pick you, Zach, I picked Pax. I am producing Pax's record, not your record. Zach, unfortunately, you are the first to go. Parker will be the drummer on this album. Keith and Trent, if you can't adequately perform with Parker, you will be the next to go."

The guys stood in silence, absorbing what had just been said. Parker watched Pax and started the countdown; she knew what was coming.

"Well, I can't sing without Zach. I refuse to record this album without him. He's been with us since the beginning. We're a package deal," Pax said as he looked at Keith, Trent, and Zach, all of them nodding at his words.

"I don't know what to tell you, Pax," Brynn said, "You are being given a once in a lifetime opportunity here, to get your music out to the world. There are others waiting to take your place if you don't want it. That's your decision. But, if I am producing this record, putting my name on it, it will be good, it will be the best I can do for you. Parker will be the drummer on this album, she will not become a member of your band. Once this is done, Parker is gone. In the meantime, Zach, you can try to get your shit together. You can take some lessons or just work to improve your skills. Once Parker is gone, you will still be the drummer for the band."

Brynn waited a moment for those words to sink in. "So, Pax, what's it going to be? You have exactly ten minutes to decide. If it's yes, then let's get to work. If it's no, pack up your shit and get going, there really is someone else waiting to take your spot here."

The guys gathered into a tight circle. Voices were raised. It was chaos for a couple of minutes. Then Pax took over the conversation, he spoke in a low, soothing voice. They finally broke apart. Pax turned to Brynn. "We'll do it your way," he said.

"Okay," she said. "Into the studio then." She pointed to the door from the booth into the studio.

Parker stood and stepped in front of Zach who was headed out the door.

"Hey, why don't you stick around," she said.

Zach was mad, he glared at her. "What for? So you can gloat about taking my place?"

"Bro, it's nothing personal. I don't care if you stay or go but your band still needs you. They need your support. If you leave it's going to put a damper on the session, they're going to be bummed. If you stay, you can see how this works, maybe learn something new. Stay for them, Zach. They do still need you."

He looked down at his feet and shrugged his shoulders.

"C'mon, stay, man," Parker encouraged him, putting a hand on his shoulder.

"Okay," he mumbled.

"Parker," Brynn said.

"Yeah," she replied. "Let's fucking do this."

She went into the studio, sat behind the kit, arranged it so it fit her.

"We good?" Brynn asked as she leaned toward the microphone connecting the booth and the studio.

Everyone nodded.

"Good. Pax, we're going to just start with you. Sing the song once. If you need some music, Keith, just guitar. I want to hear it stripped down. Then we'll do it again right away. Parker, you can pick up in the second round."

That was like twelve hours ago. This was nothing new to Parker, sessions usually went for hours but this was a little longer than normal. The band was vibing, they were high with recording their music. Keith and Trent were pulling their weight but not perfect. There were moments of absolute genius but also total fuck-ups.

Brynn was true to her word. That was the last take. Parker called Tony to pick her up while she tried to dry off. The band was still in the studio, with Zach, Brynn, and the tech. They were laughing and high-fiving each other while drinking beer. Parker went to join them while waiting for Tony. She uncapped a beer and took a long pull.

Zach approached her. "Thanks for getting me to stay," he said.

"No problem, Zach," she said. "The band was happy to have you here. It made things better for everyone just because you were here."

"Yeah, I see that."

Brynn spoke from her left shoulder. "Fuck, it's good to see you again, Parker."

Parker smiled. "Likewise, Mighty Brynn Star Maker."

"Oh stop. So, what's with you and the billionaire, what's his name again?"

"Mickey Finn. Nothing, he's actually Toby Finn's brother. I was on tour with Temptation when their drummer had his appendix removed. We stopped here and I met him. Right now, he's just a place to stay. A really nice place to stay."

"Really? That's all?" Brynn smirked at her. "I've seen the pics, girlfriend."

Parker's phone vibrated. She pulled it out of her coat pocket at looked at it. "My ride's here, Brynn. See you tomorrow."

"Yeah, tomorrow."

$$$

Parker was soaking in a hot tub, letting her muscles relax. She was disappointed that she got home so late. Mickey was sleeping. *Probably naked and just next door,* she thought to herself and smiled, as she slid under the water.

CHAPTER 10
Mickey

He was in the car on the way to work, scrolling through his emails.

"What time did you pick her up?" he asked Tony.

"She called at midnight. I had her home by one-ish," he responded. "You know, that little girl can eat!"

Mickey met his eyes in the rear-view mirror, his eyebrow raised.

"We went through a drive thru on the way home. Two double cheeseburgers and a large fries." Tony chuckled and shook his head. "She was eating in the car. Couldn't wait to get home."

Mickey smiled to himself as he opened an email from the mayor.

$$$

His morning had been busy. He'd met with his project manager over breakfast to discuss ground breaking and subcontractors for the Village project. Once in the office he was on the phone with his property manager to discuss lease up of the mall in Potter's Creek. He ended that call at 9:30 and called his assistant into his office. His cell phone pinged. It was a text from Parker. He smiled as he read it.

Parker: *Hey, Rod. Second morning in a row I didn't see you. World domination going well?*

Mickey: *Early bird gets the worm, sleepyhead. How was the studio?*

Parker: *It was long. Hopefully not so long today. Maybe I'll see you later.*

Mickey: *Miss me? Just curious.*

Parker: *Miss the scenery. Hubba hubba.*

Mickey: *Does your mom know you speak to guys like that?*

Parker: *Is it hard to sit with your wallet full of so many billions of dollars. Ahwooga.*

Mickey: *Sometimes, the world always seems to be on a tilt. Not sure why.*

Parker: *Topic for discussion later. Gotta go. Just pulled up to the studio.*

Mickey: *Give em hell, baby.*

Parker: *Always do. You should know.*

$$$

So, the day went longer than expected. He didn't get home until midnight. Tony informed him that he had picked up Parker around seven that night. He wondered if she was still awake as he walked into the house, pulling his tie off and undoing the top button of his shirt.

The house was dark, lit only by the under-cupboard lights in the kitchen. He put his case on the island and walked down the hall to Parker's room. It was quiet, no light shone from under her door. He pushed his fingers through his hair. He had really wanted to see her tonight, spend some time with her. Instead, he continued down the hall to his room, closing the door behind him, to prepare for bed.

$$$

The rest of the week was a carbon copy. Parker worked into the evening or he had something come up at the last minute, that kept him busy into the night. He went to work early in the morning, she didn't get out of bed until after he had gone. It was Friday already.

Mickey: *Do you have plans for Saturday night?*

Parker: *No, have the weekend off.*

Mickey: *I have a thing Saturday night. Want to come?*

Parker: *A thing?*

Mickey: *A charity event, involving dinner and a big cheque.*

Parker: *Will there be cake?*

Mickey: *Can't confirm that.*

Parker: *No cake? Hmmmmm…*

Mickey: *We can go for cake after.*

Parker: *Do you promise?*

Mickey: *I swear.*

Parker: *You know, I don't have anything fancy to wear.*

Mickey: *Not a problem, baby. You know I've got you.*

Parker: *That should be interesting. Gotta go. Just got here.*

$$$

Another long night. Mickey blew out the breath he had been holding. He had wanted to see Parker tonight, maybe have dinner together, but something came up and he found himself in the office until almost midnight.

He walked into his dark, quiet house; the hallway lit only by the under-cupboard lights in the kitchen. He walked into the living area and was surprised to see the lamp on the end table beside the couch was on, casting a low glow. He loosened his tie and went to turn it off.

Parker was asleep on the couch, curled on her side with a book on the floor. He smiled as he watched her sleep. He reached out his hand and put his palm on her cheek. She stirred at his touch and rolled onto her back. She brought her hand up to cover his and rubbed her cheek against his palm. Something tightened in his stomach.

Her eyes fluttered open and focused on his face. She smiled up at him. "Mickey Finn," she whispered.

"The one and only," he responded, quietly smiling down at her.

Their eyes locked. Everything else faded into the background. Parker grabbed his tie in her hand and pulled, pulling him down, over the back of the couch and on top of her. She opened her legs to accommodate him and wrapped them around his waist as he settled on top of her, his elbows on the couch supporting his weight. His cock hardened against her thigh.

Mickey's eyes blazed into hers. "Is this wise, Parker?" he asked.

Her hands lifted to his neck and skimmed into his hair. She grabbed his hair and brought his face down to hers. He stopped, his lips inches from her mouth. "Is this what you want?" he asked again.

She responded by pushing her hips up against him and shimmying so that his cock was resting on her pussy. She pushed up again, rubbing herself against the seam of her shorts and the hardness of his cock. She did it again.

Mickey pulsed against her. Fuck. She looked at him through lidded eyes. She pulled his face down and kissed him, her tongue probing at his lips until he opened his mouth. She pushed her hips against him again as she plunged her tongue into his mouth, tasting him.

She began to ride his cock, she wanted him.

Mickey felt the need in her and responded. She wasn't the only one who didn't want to wait for this. He wrapped his arms around her and shifted until she was sitting on top of him. His hands spanned her waist as he watched the determined look on her face as she rode him.

She glanced down at his eyes, which were burning into her. She reached down and pulled her T-shirt over her head. She unclasped her bra and threw it on the floor. She took his hands in hers and placed them on her breasts.

They fit his hands perfectly, as he knew they would. He squeezed her roughly. She moaned under his touch. His hands went back to her waist. He picked her up. He sat up and put her on his lap, her back resting against his chest. He reclaimed her breast with one hand, the other hand going down to her shorts and unsnapping the button. She began to squirm on his lap, the friction from her shorts lost, her desire still peaking.

Mickey slid his hand under her shorts down her

stomach. He nibbled at her neck, breathing heavily into her ear. His fingers found the elastic of her panties. He moved her legs to the outside of his thighs and spread her open with his legs. One hand returned to her breast, pinching and tugging at her nipple. The other hand slid under her shorts, under her panties and into her wet pussy. He moaned into her neck.

"Is this what you want, baby? My hands on your body? You have great tits." He pinched her nipple and her chest thrust out. "And this pussy," he growled, "it's soaking wet." Roughly, he ran his fingers in between her lips. "Is this pussy wet for me, baby?"

She moaned. She tried to squeeze her thighs together but his legs held her wide open. She whimpered with her need. "Yes, Mickey, yes."

"Yes what, baby?" He teased her, skimming his fingers between her lips and over her clit. "Is this mine? Is this for me?"

"Yes," she breathed. "Yes." She put her hand over his hand, pushing him against her as she squirmed. Trying to get his hand to stop moving. "Please, Mickey, please," she begged.

Finally, his fingers stopped on her clit. He circled her nub. She was so wet his fingers easily slid over her. He pushed down, rubbing her as she rode his hand, moving her hips and moaning. "That's it, baby, this is for you. You know I've got you." He maneuvered his hand so his thumb continued to rub her clit as he slid two fingers into her.

"Oh my…" She couldn't finish as she gave into the pleasure running rampant through her body. He kissed her neck, breathing into her ear as he pulled and pinched her nipple and slid his fingers in and out of her while rubbing her clit.

"I want you to come for me, baby. I want to feel you come on my fingers," he whispered into her neck. "Tell me who makes you feel so good." He stuck his tongue in her ear.

She shot off like a rocket, all engines firing. He felt her clench around his fingers. Her body tightened and she arched against his chest. "Say my name, baby, say it," he demanded.

"Mickey," she sobbed as he continued to rub her clit and pinch her nipple.

"That's right, baby," he whispered into her neck. He released her. He took his hand out of her shorts and brought his legs together. He picked her up again and turned her so that she was straddling him on the couch. She sagged against him, her cheek resting on his chest. He rubbed her warm back.

They sat in silence, enjoying the feel of their bodies resting against each other. Mickey stood, his hands under her ass as he carried her down the hall, fully intending to put her where she belonged.

In his bed.

CHAPTER 11
Parker

Mickey carried her into his bedroom. He took her shorts off and, leaving her in her panties, lifted the covers for her to slide into his bed.

She watched as he walked into his closet and began to strip—his tie first and then his shirt. He had unbuckled his belt and pulled it free of his pants, placing it on the island. He undid his pants and stepped out of them, one leg at a time. He placed them over a chair and then slid his socks off. He wore only a pair of tight black knit boxers that hugged his ass. He turned toward her and she caught a glimpse of the bulge in front of him before he switched off the light.

He slid into bed beside her. She lay rigidly beside him. This was awkward. This is where things usually started for her, then when it was done, she was getting up and leaving. This was different, they were already done and this is where they ended up. She had never spent the night with a man under these circumstances and was not sure what to do.

Mickey reached over and pulled her against him. He felt the tension in her body. He took her hand and put it on his chest. He rubbed her back and kissed her forehead before placing his hand on top of hers. His breathing was strong and steady, she felt his heart beating beneath her palm. It wasn't long before his breathing slowed and deepened. He was asleep and it was not long after that she drifted off.

$$\$\$\$$$

She got out of bed and went into her room to shower and change. She put on a new pair of panties and the T-shirt he had given her on her first night here.

She walked into the living area. Mickey was at the island, as expected. His chest bare, paper in one hand, coffee cup in another. He looked up at her and smiled.

"Morning, baby. Sleep well?"

"Yes, thank you." She smiled back at him, suddenly shy and blushing.

She got her coffee, went to the fridge for cream, closed the door and leaned against it to enjoy the spectacular view she usually got on the mornings that Mickey was home. She laughed. No sweatpants today, only his tight boxers hugging his incredible ass. He swiveled the stool toward her.

"No pants today, Rod?"

"You know that's my T-shirt."

"Not anymore. It's mine now."

He smirked at her and swiveled back to the island with his coffee and the paper.

Parker took a few sips of coffee, leaning against the

fridge, her eyes closed. She walked to the other side of the island and picked up the lifestyle section of the paper. She stared at the front page, not really seeing the words. She put the paper down and looked at Mickey.

He glanced up at her, her coffee cup in front of her mouth, looked back at the paper and then back at her. He seemed to be surprised at the heat in her gaze and then he smirked. He put his paper down, stood and walked around the island. He stopped behind her, placing his hands on her shoulders.

She swiveled around to face him and lifted her chin, inviting his kiss. He bent down and brushed his lips against hers.

"Tell me what you want, baby."

She met his eyes. "You," she responded.

He took the hem of her T-shirt and lifted it off of her when she raised her arms. He picked her up and placed her on the island before bending down and taking her nipple in his mouth, licking it, swirling his tongue around it until it peaked. She put her hands in his hair, holding his head to her chest. He sucked her nipple hard and drew it slowly out of his mouth before turning to her other nipple, repeating the process.

He leaned his hands on the island and leaned into her taking her lips in his. "Is that good, baby? Do you want more?"

She ran her hands over his body: his strong shoulders, down his arms, over his chest and abs, down to the waist of his boxers.

He stopped her, taking her hands in his and bringing

them up to his lips. He placed her hands on either side of her body on the island and then put his fingers into the waistband of her panties. She lifted herself off the island long enough for him to slide her panties down her thighs. He dropped them on the kitchen floor.

He put his forehead against hers, breathing heavily. "You are so beautiful," he said. "I have wanted you like this from the moment you walked into my house." He took in a deep breath, steadying himself. "Open your legs for me, baby, let me see you."

His words and the tone of his voice made her wet. A thrill ran from her pussy through her entire body. She spread her legs for him.

He looked down at her. He slid one finger between her lips, covering it with her wetness. He brought it up to his face, smelling his finger before sliding it into his mouth. "I'm going to eat my fill and then I am going to fuck you until you scream my name."

He put his hands on her thighs and spread them even wider. With his fingers he spread her lips. He leaned forward and blew against her. She arched her back, moaning as her nipples peaked. Still spreading her lips apart, he slowly slid one finger into her, then a second finger. He pulled his fingers out, bent forward putting his face into her pussy and licked her. He licked her from her clit, through her folds, from the top of her pussy to the bottom and then back again.

Okay, this was nice, Parker thought. Then he sucked her clit and she fell back on the island. Holy. Shit. Mickey started to fuck her with his tongue, his finger joining the party, rubbing her clit. Parker squirmed on the island, trying to bring her legs together but Mickey held her open as he continued the assault on her pussy. She put her hands in his hair, pushing his face into her, holding him there. She began to grind her hips into his face, he circled her clit with his tongue then slid his fingers into her, hooking them to find her G-spot. He sucked her clit one more time before she arched her back off the island, coming on his face.

He stood and looked down at her, watching as the pleasure took her body. He continued to rub her clit with his finger, waiting for her orgasm to end. She lay spread out for him on the island. Her arms were over her head, clutching the other side of the granite top, her back was arched off the island, her tits thrust up, her nipples hard and her legs were spread wide, her pussy glistening from his ministrations.

"You are beautiful, baby," he rasped. "I'm going to fuck you so hard. Are you ready for my cock to be inside of you?"

He pushed the waistband of his boxers down, releasing his cock. It sprung free of the fabric, bobbing against him. He leaned forward and found the condom that he had brought with him this morning. He ripped the package open, slid it over his length and plunged into her wetness.

Parker screamed as he pushed into her. He was so big and thick and good. She had never been filled like this. He fucked her hard and fast, leaning over her, watching her face, his jaw set. "You know you like it," he ground out. "This cock is for you. It's yours now, baby." He pounded in and out of her, watching as her tits bounced with every thrust. He put one hand on her hip, with his other he grasped her wrists and held them over her head. He had no control. He was lost in her. He couldn't stop to savor her body. He couldn't get enough of her. Sliding in and out of her wet softness was too good, he wouldn't be able to hold on for long.

She started to clench his cock. He looked down at her. Her face was flushed, her eyes half closed. "Come for me, baby. You know you want to. Come on my cock as I'm fucking you." He leaned forward and took a nipple into his mouth, sucking and slowly sliding it out of his mouth. "Who does this pussy belong to? Who's going to give you this big hard cock? Tell me, baby…"

He slammed into her again and again. She came with a scream, her pussy clenching around him. "Say it, baby, say my name," he demanded.

"OH MY GOD, MICKEY," she screamed. "MICKEY."

Then he lost it. He exploded inside of her. He fell on top of her, hot and sweating. Pulling himself together, he propped himself up on his elbows. She gazed into his eyes, then put her arms around his neck. He stood pulling her up with him. He put his hands under her ass and carried her into his bedroom, into the en suite, into the shower.

He turned it on, the warm water running down their bodies. He stayed inside her until he hardened again. He propped her up against the shower wall and fucked her again until they both came. He stepped out of the shower, disposed of the condom and went back in. They washed each other, their hands gliding over their soapy bodies.

They dried each other off before snuggling under the covers of his bed until they both fell asleep.

CHAPTER 12
Parker

When she woke, Mickey was still wrapped around her, one arm across her chest, his leg over hers. She lay still, enjoying his weight on her, thinking over the morning and smiling. Fuck, she felt good. She couldn't recall the number of times he had made her come. He knew how to play her body to get it to respond, her neck, her nipples, her pussy were all his instruments. Just thinking of him pounding into her on the kitchen island got her wet again.

"What are you thinking about?" his deep voice quietly asked.

"Oh, you know," she said.

"Tell me anyway." He rolled onto his side so that he was looking at her, watching her.

She blushed. He leaned over and kissed her gently on the mouth.

"I'm hungry," she said, ignoring his request, "bordering on hangry, and let me tell you, Mickey Finn, that is not something you want to see."

"What do you want to do? Cook? Eat out? Order in?"

She loved that he always offered her those options.

"Let's cook. Eggs and toast are fast and easy. Do you have any bacon or ham?"

"Not sure what I have in the fridge, let's look."

He lifted the cover and rolled out of bed, groaning. "If you hadn't threatened me with hangry violence, I would have kept you in here all day, you know that, don't you?"

"You are awful," she said. "The proper care and maintenance of a girl includes feeding her regularly, you know that, don't you?"

He pulled on his boxers and stood, holding his hand out to her. She took his hand and pulled herself out of bed. "My clothes are still in the kitchen," she said as she walked past him.

He reached out and gave her ass a slap. "You're playing with fire, baby. You better get something on or you won't be eating anything for another hour."

Parker shrieked and ran ahead of him into the kitchen. She scooped up her panties, grabbed the T-shirt, and pulled it over her head as she rounded the island. She quickly stepped into her panties and opened the fridge door just as Mickey entered the room.

"Oh hey, there are lots of things in here. We can have an omelette," she said as she started pulling vegetables out of the fridge and putting them on the counter.

Mickey pulled out two chopping boards and knives. They both set to peeling and chopping the ingredients for the omelette. Parker pulled out a frying pan to sauté the vegetables before adding the eggs and cheese. When it was done, she flipped the omelette onto a dinner plate which they shared sitting beside each other.

When brunch was done, they both cleaned the kitchen. Mickey went to his office to check his emails and make some calls. Parker picked her book up from the living room floor and sat on the couch reading. An hour later, Mickey came out of his office and they snuggled on the couch watching a movie.

"We should start getting ready," he said as the movie credits rolled. "We should leave in another hour or so."

"Oh no! I still don't have anything to wear," Parker said. "I thought…"

"I told you I would get you something, baby. Come with me." He took her hand and led her into his bedroom.

"Don't think I'm going to fall for the 'come into my bedroom to get your new clothes' trick, Rod." She laughed up at him.

"Am I so transparent?"

"Like glass."

He cupped her chin, bent down and kissed her. "If only that trick would work but, no, that is not the plan. Come." He led her into his closet and pulled a garment bag down from where it had been hanging. "Here," he said. "This should do the trick."

She took the bag from his hands. "I'm going to get dressed in my room."

"This is your room," he growled at her.

"My other room, silly." She kissed him again before leaving him to get dressed.

$$$

She came down the hallway, sparkling in her dress. She entered the living area and found Mickey in his tuxedo, looking down at his phone. He took her breath away. He was in a black tuxedo with a crisp white button-down shirt and black bow tie. He put his phone down and turned to look at her, his eyes taking her in from head to toe.

"I like it. You look beautiful," he said as he held his hand out to her.

He had picked a short cocktail dress with spaghetti straps that came down to mid-thigh. It was adorned with short strings of silver beads that swayed and sparkled as she walked. She loved it but it felt a little too simple for her. She had added a short black leather moto jacket that ended just below her bustline and her black Doc Martens, laces untied. Her hair, as usual, was stylishly messy. Her makeup simple.

When she put out her hand to take his, he slid a long black velvet box into her palm. She pulled her hand back and looked down at the box. She looked up at him. He was smiling. "I thought of you when I saw this," he said.

"You really didn't have to, Mickey."

"Yes, I did. Open it, baby."

She slowly opened the case. Her breath caught in her throat when she saw what was in there.

"I can't accept this, Mickey."

He reached into the box and pulled out a simple diamond choker. He stood behind her as he put it around her neck and fastened the clasp in the back. "You have to accept this Parker, it's a gift. From me to you." He put his hands on her shoulders and leaned forward to nuzzle her neck.

She turned in his arms, her lips meeting his. "It's beautiful. Thank you."

$$$

He held her hand as they walked the red carpet into the event. When they stopped for photos he put his arm around her shoulder, pulling her into his side. The picture of them in the paper tomorrow was one where they were looking at each other smiling.

They entered the ballroom and someone called his name. He found the source of the voice and smiled. He pulled her along with him toward a group of people standing near one of the bars set up around the room. He quickly placed a drink order with the bartender before turning to the group.

"Gentlemen," he greeted them. "Haven't seen you since the last event."

"Mickey Finn," a tall blond man with a well-groomed beard and mustache said, as he held out his hand. "Been busy. We need to set a date to get together. It's been too long."

"Way too long, but you know how things are, busy, busy," another man said, slapping Mickey on the shoulder but meeting Parker's eyes with a smile.

A man with a light blue turban looked at her as he took Mickey's hand. "Who's your friend Mickey?" he asked.

"Gents, this is Parker Chen," he introduced her. "Parker, this is Darshan," he introduced the fellow wearing the turban, "Paul," the man with the beard, "and Sven," the tall blond. "We all went to university together although I've known Darshan since high school.

"Parker Chen. Certainly not Parker Chen on the *Blue* album?" Darshan asked.

"One and the same," Parker responded.

"Oh my God. It's an absolute honor to meet you," he gushed, as he took her hand in his. "What are you doing here with this buffoon?"

Parker laughed. "Brynn Williams is here producing an album. I'm playing on it."

"Have I gone to heaven? Brynn Williams is in the city, too?" Darshan looked at Paul, Sven and Mickey. "Do you guys even know who Brynn Williams is? Or Parker for that matter? Parker is one of the greatest drummers of all time," he still held her hand in his, "and Brynn Williams has produced more Grammy award albums than any other producer in the past ten years."

"Okay, Darshan. Let's dial down the fanboy enthusiasm a bit," Mickey said as he pulled Parker's hand out of his, reclaiming her.

"She still hasn't answered my question about you. What are you doing with this buffoon?"

All eyes were on her as she smiled up at Mickey. "I kinda like him," she responded as she lifted her chin toward him.

Mickey bent down and brushed his lips across hers, pausing as they looked into each other's eyes. His friends exchanged looks; Sven rolled his eyes.

"Yeah," Mickey finally looked at Sven, "how's the hotel

business, Sven? Thought anymore about committing to my Village project?"

"My team is running the numbers, Mickey. We should have something to talk about in a couple weeks," Sven said.

"How is the Village project coming along?" Paul asked. "Last time we spoke you hadn't closed with Benson."

"Yeah, closed that about three, four weeks ago. I'm meeting with the engineers to get the plans and specs done up. That's going to be another month or two."

The bartender placed two glasses of white wine on the counter. Mickey picked up the glasses and passed one to Parker.

"Finn," a voice called from behind them.

Mickey turned and greeted another man who was also known to all the other men in this group. They continued talking about the Village project. Parker looked around the ballroom. There was a big band playing jazz on a stage at the front of the room.

"This must be boring for you," Darshan said at her side.

She looked at him as she sipped her wine. "Kind of. These things generally are. I'm certainly not into land development, although what Mickey has told me about his Village project, it seems to be pretty exciting."

"So, tell me about this album you are working on," he encouraged her.

She told him about how Brynn had agreed to produce a record for the winner of a contest as PR for a new studio. He peppered her with questions about Brynn, then about some of the other artists she had worked with. They were laughing over a story about a major recording artist that Parker was sharing when a hand rested on her lower back.

Mickey leaned to whisper in her ear, "Enjoying yourself baby?"

She nodded her head and put her arm around his waist, giving him a squeeze. "You should come down to the studio, Darshan. You can meet Brynn."

"I'd love to, Parker," he enthused.

She reached over and plucked his phone out of his suit breast pocket. She opened the contacts and entered her number. "That's me," she said as she handed it back to him. "Call or text when you have time and we can set something up. It has to be within the next three weeks, four at the most. The album will probably be done by then and I'll be on my way back to L.A."

"I'll keep that in mind," Darshan said, smiling at her. He looked at Mickey and his smile quickly died. "Hey, strictly on the level, man," he said as he put this phone back in his breast pocket and went to the bar to order another drink.

Parker turned into him, putting her arms around him, placing her chin on his chest and looking up at him. "What's with the stink eye, Rod. You are going to scare everyone away."

He smirked at her. "Just looking after what's...you," he said.

She kept her arm around his waist as they walked through the ballroom to the silent auction prizes where he bought twenty tickets and gave them to her. She spent time looking at all the prizes, putting her tickets into the boxes for the prizes she wanted.

She felt his eyes on her. She finally turned toward him holding out her hand. "Mickey, would you go for a couples massage with me? We would get matching robes," she said.

"Of course, baby," he said as he brought her hand to his lips, kissing it.

"Well, aren't you two the sweetest things here," a woman's voice spoke from behind them.

Parker's eyes darted to those of a petite woman with silver hair dressed in green satin.

"Lucinda," Mickey greeted her. "I was hoping we wouldn't see you here tonight."

"Oh posh, Mickey. You know I always come to these things. Always need to have my nose to the ground for the next story." She was speaking to Mickey but her eyes were assessing Parker. "Who is your friend, Mickey? We've seen a lot of you two, but I don't think I have ever met her."

"Lucinda, Parker Chen. Parker, this is Lucinda Sturgis. She writes the gossip column in the *Sentinel*."

"A pleasure, Parker." She held out her hand. "Parker, such an unusual name." Lucinda turned her gaze to Mickey. "So, is this serious, Mickey? Something I should know about?"

Parker laughed. "Serious? I've only fucked him a couple of times, Lucy, I don't even know how he takes his coffee."

"That's Lucinda, dear," she said tersely, before turning on her heel and storming away.

"Black," Mickey said. "I take my coffee black."

$$$

Parker didn't know if Mickey was mad at her and, frankly, she didn't care. She didn't mind having her picture splashed across the page but don't ask any personal questions, as if she would answer them. Besides, there was no "serious" when it came to her and Mickey. She wasn't ready to be tied down and, apparently, he didn't date anyone more than once. She knew she was already on borrowed time with him.

They were standing in yet another group discussing the Village project. She thought she had been introduced to the Mayor and some councilmen, but she wasn't sure who they were. Anyway, her glass was empty. She pulled her hand out of Mickey's and made her way to the closest bar. Leaning against the counter she placed her order when someone said:

"P-P-P-Parker Ch-Ch-Chen, c'mon down."

There was only one person who said her name like that. She squealed with delight and flew into a man's arms. "B-B-B-Barney B-B-Blum!"

He hugged her tightly before releasing her and holding her at arm's length. "What the holy fuck are you doing here?" he asked.

"I asked you first, Barney," she teased, a huge grin on her face, falling into an old game of theirs.

"I'm with the band, sweetheart. Didn't you notice my saxophone stylings while you were hobnobbing with the rich and famous? Don't answer that! I am already wounded."

"I'm doing some studio work for Brynn Williams," she

spit out. "Oh my God! I am so happy to see you," she said as she fell into his arms again.

Barney threw his head back and laughed before kissing her on the forehead. "I've missed you, too, Parker," he said. Suddenly, he froze and released her. Smiling, he asked through his clenched lips, "Do you know that guy?"

Parker turned to find Mickey glaring at Barney. What the fuck?

"Mickey, this is Barney Blum. We went to Julliard together," she introduced him. "Barney is playing with the band." She waved her hand toward the stage.

Mickey held out his hand. "Pleasure to meet you, Barney."

Hesitantly, Barney shook his hand. "It's all good, man, just really good friends who haven't seen each other in a long time."

Mickey seemed to relax at that.

"We used to get so drunk on cheap wine," Parker giggled, "remember? You, me, Tanya, and Carl."

"Girl, don't even, I still get nauseous when I think about after our finals."

Parker laughed. "You were soooo drunk." She took Mickey's hand and then put her arm around his waist, laughing into his side. Mickey slid his hand up her arm and rested it on her shoulder. "How did we ever drift apart, Barney?"

"Who knows…" he said.

"And who cares," they said in unison before breaking into laughter.

Barney looked past Parker's shoulder. "Looks like the

troops are gathering," he said. He pulled his phone out of his jacket pocket and gave it to her. "Put in your deets, Parker."

She took his phone and entered the number. Then she called herself. "And now I have your number," she said. "Let's do coffee in the next couple of weeks. I'm only here for another three or four weeks."

"It's a date, Parkie." They hugged one last time before he hurried off to the stage.

Mickey looked down at her shining face. "Parkie?"

Five minutes later the band started playing.

CHAPTER 13
Mickey

Okay, so he was a jealous fucker. When Parker had joked about his stink eye, he had almost told her he was just looking after what was his. Yes, Parker was his. She should know that.

He was a little miffed when she gave Darshan, one of his oldest friends by the way, her number and invited him to the studio. He could have actually killed Barney Blum until he had been introduced to him.

She was so adorable though. Her response to Lucinda still made him smile and the way she kept hugging him and asking for kisses, she was so natural with her affection for him.

But, really, what the fuck, she had said more than once that she would only be here for another three or four weeks. That was a problem, a big fucking problem.

$$\$\$\$$$

They were in the back of the car, Parker snuggled up against his side. "You promised me cake, Mr. Finn," she said sternly. "Do you remember having any cake this evening?"

"No," he said as he nuzzled her neck. "You are sweet enough for me, baby."

"Don't you baby me, you sweet talker. Cake was promised."

He pulled her onto his lap, his hand on her knee. "Where do you want to go for cake?" His hand slid up her leg, under the hem of her dress. His lips were on her neck, trailing down to the top of her dress.

She pulled his hand off her leg. "You tell me, Rod. Where can we get cake around here at this time?"

He sighed heavily. He leaned forward and pressed a button. "Tony, take us to the club."

He put his hand back on her knee, sliding it up her leg, under her dress. "We have fifteen minutes until it's cake time. Can you wait that long?"

She smiled a wicked smile at him. He raised his eyebrows. She slid off his lap and across the seat, to the farthest side of the car. She leaned toward him and undid his belt.

"Baby," he moaned, "what are you doing?"

"This time, I've got you, baby," she said as she popped the button on his pants and slid the zipper down.

"Do you know what I am going to do for you, Rod?"

"I have a pretty good idea," he panted.

"Just lean back and relax," she said as she reached into his pants and pulled out his cock.

Parker gripped him and leaned forward to lick his head. She pursed her lips and slid them over his head, the fit was tight. One of Mickey's hands went into her hair, the other on her neck. He pulsed his hips up into her mouth.

She popped him out of her mouth. She looked at him and ran her tongue around her mouth, over her lips. She winked at him and went down again. She slid him all the way into her mouth, opening her throat to allow all of him to enter. She pulled up slowly, looking up at him. His eyes were closed, his jaw clenched.

She slid down his length again, sucking all the way down and back up again. She stroked his length with a tight fist, causing him to jerk his hips into her hand. She put her mouth on him again, slid her hand into his pants and cupped his balls, massaging them. He moaned.

She picked up her pace, sliding his thick cock in and out of her mouth, sucking to cause the friction needed. She massaged his balls in time with her movements. He gripped her hair and started pumping into her mouth. He was doing all the work now, she was applying the pressure and massaging his balls. She felt them tighten in her hand. She pushed her mouth all the way down to his root and stayed there. He pushed into her mouth twice more before he shot his cum down her throat. She swallowed it all.

He was a wet rag, collapsed against the back seat of the car. He looked at her and smiled as she sat up, ran her finger around her lips, put it into her mouth and licked it clean. He almost came again when she did that. He probably would have but she had milked him dry.

$$$

"Just the dessert menu," Mickey told the waiter when he appeared at the table.

He held her hand, bringing it up to his lips and kissing her knuckles.

The waiter returned with the dessert cart, describing the selections available. Looking into her eyes, Mickey ordered one of everything. Parker giggled. It was music to his ears. He wanted her to be happy. He wanted to be the one to make her happy. It was only fair to return the favor because she sure as hell made him happy.

Their table was covered with dessert plates. They each had a fork. They were in a private room. He pulled Parker onto his knee and fed her cake until all the plates were empty. Then he put his hands on each side of her head and pulled her down to him for a kiss. Parker clung to him, responding to the passion in his kiss.

He sensed the waiter come in, discreetly put the bill on the table and leave. He finally ended the kiss. The waiter appeared and Mickey paid the bill, leaving him a substantial tip for his discretion.

"Let's go home," he growled at her, pulling her behind him into the car.

$$$

They kissed from the car up the walkway, not breaking while Mickey fumbled for his keys and opened the door. He carried her, her legs wrapped around his waist into the house, down the hallway and into his bedroom. He placed her gently on his bed and watched as they both stripped.

She took off her moto jacket and kicked off her boots. He undid his bowtie and pulled it off, dropping it on the floor, his tuxedo jacket was the next article added to his pile. She stood, slipped the straps of her dress off her shoulders and let it drop to the floor. He removed his shirt, then opened his pants and stepped out of them. She stepped out of her thong and stood before him naked. He pulled down his boxers and stepped out of them, sliding off his socks.

He was on her instantly. He pulled her to him and claimed her lips as he laid her on his bed. He couldn't wait. He grabbed a condom, slid it on, spread her legs and entered her. She was already wet and welcomed him, pulling her knees up to her chest. He sank into her, pulled back and drove into her again. She moaned.

Her arms were over her head, he grabbed her wrists and held them down. His other hand was on her hip, pinning her to the bed. He dropped his head and sucked her nipples, first one then the other, all while he plowed into her.

"Do you know who this pussy belongs to, baby?" he asked as he drove into her. "Tell me."

"You," her breath shuddered out.

"Fucking right. Who's job is it to fuck this pussy?"

"Yours."

"Who wants this cock in their pussy, baby?"

"I do…Mickey?"

"I know, I know you're going to come. Who do you come for?"

"You, Mickey, you."

"That's right." He pushed into her, feeling her orgasm

clench his cock. "That pussy is mine, baby. Mine," he shouted as he came inside her.

$$$

Mickey was between her thighs, licking her slowly. She moaned with pleasure. Her eyes popped open and looked down to meet his. She smiled as he reached up and took one of her breasts in his hand, massaging it. She lay back down, reaching up and grabbing the head board while he worked on her.

Mickey was in no rush and neither was she. She spread her legs wider for him. She played with her nipples, enjoying the feeling of her orgasm building. He slowly fucked her pussy with his tongue as he lazily circled her clit with his finger.

She tasted so good. He was getting as much pleasure as she was by playing with her. He stopped his ministrations, reached for a condom, spooned her and slid into her from behind. He held her against his body, one hand rubbing her clit while the other held her forehead back against him so he could nuzzle her neck.

She began to squirm, pushing her ass against him. He knelt behind her, pulling her ass up against him as he moved. She was on all fours on the bed. He quickened his pace, pushing into her, responding to her request. They came together. He collapsed on top of her before rolling off. He lay beside her, sweating, his hand on his chest, breathing deeply.

CHAPTER 14
Parker

She rolled onto her back beside him in his bed. She turned her head, looking at him, at his handsome face, at the smile there. She put that there.

Suddenly she realized that he was hers as much as he demanded that she was his. Following that astounding realization was that she was starting to care about him, like *really* care about him.

Yeah, she had to shut that shit down. She was only going to be here for another few weeks and then she was gone back to L.A. She just hoped that his interest in her would last that long. Sure, she could move back into her room but that would be awkward. When he tired of her, like he seemed to tire of all his women, she would just rent a room at the Fairmont like she had originally planned. In any event, it was going to hurt. If she allowed this...whatever it was...to continue, it would really hurt.

She was such an idiot. She knew all along that she should not have started something with him until she was closer to leaving. That was the original plan, but no,

Fucking Mickey Finn happened. He had slipped under her guard, past all her defences, and shot all her plans to hell.

Nope. Can't happen. She slid out of bed, picked up her clothes and headed next door to the guest room.

Mickey watched her. "Where are you going?"

"To take a shower and get dressed," she responded, a little coldly.

She took her time in the shower, letting the water beat down on her as she planned how to move forward from here:

Cut off the best sex of her life? *Kind of late for that, don't you think?* she asked herself. Yeah.

You don't really want to do that anyway. No.

Avoid him? *Can't today, it's Sunday, and we just had a great Friday and Saturday.* Ah, no.

Pick a fight? *Even more awkward and leading to make-up sex or moving out.* Yeah, no.

She leaned her head against the shower tile. She knew who would be able to tell her what to do. She knew who would know how to handle this man and, really, any man. She closed her eyes and asked herself, *What would my mother do?*

$$$

She came into the living area to find Mickey at his station, behind the island with a coffee and the paper, looking as hot as ever. This time when he looked up at her with a smile on his face, she snarled back at him, more angry at herself than him.

She stomped over to the coffee station and poured a cup, then to the fridge for cream. She closed the fridge door a little too forcefully before sitting at the island across from him, grabbing the lifestyle section of the paper and holding it up to shield her face from his view.

Aaaand…what was on the front page of the section? A picture of her and Mickey at the event last night. God, she looked like she had stars in her eyes! He was smiling down at her like he knew he was going to get the best blow job of his life later that night. If she didn't know better, she would say that they looked like they were in love.

Okay, she said to herself, *calm down!* She whipped the first page open to find another picture of her and Mickey on top of Lucinda's column. The headline read *Pot Meets Kettle*. What the…

> *The mystery is solved. Billionaire Mickey Finn's latest companion is Parker Chen. For those of you who don't know, Ms. Chen is a percussion virtuoso, a studio musician from Los Angeles, gracing our fair city with her talent while recording an album with another celebrity from L.A., homegirl, Brynn Williams. Brynn Williams is producing an album for a local band who won a contest to promote the opening of Red Dog Running Studio.*
>
> *But I digress. The hard-to-pin-down Mickey Finn may have met his match with the beautiful Parker Chen who can't seem to, or doesn't want to, hold onto her own man for more than a week at a time. The revolving door to her bedroom has seen many*

famous faces from the music world. Oh my, if her
bedsheets could talk!

One can only wonder if poor Mickey Finn knows
about his little friend's reputation. It looked like a
perfect match from the outside but it seems like the clock
is ticking down on this friendship. Who will tire first?
Mickey or Parker?

"You fucking cunt," Parker spit out before heaving her coffee cup at the kitchen wall. She watched as it hit the tile, exploding, sending shards of glass flying and coffee dripping.

Mickey startled at the explosion and looked up to see her storming out of the living area into her room.

Parker was fuming. It's not like her life was a secret, but this was the first hatchet job she had ever seen that had been levelled at her and in a newspaper. That was not cool. Did she deserve it after her exchange with Lucinda last night? Maybe.

She threw on some clothes and called Tony. She had to get out of here. She came out of her en suite to find Mickey standing in her room.

"You're mad," he said simply.

"No shit, Sherlock. You should be a detective," she snapped as she grabbed her purse.

"What are you doing?"

"I'm going out."

"Where to?"

"Anywhere but here," she stalked toward the door of her room.

Mickey reached out to grab her shoulders and make her stop. "Calm down, baby."

She shook herself out of his grasp and glared up at him. "You fucking calm down…baby," she sneered the last word at him.

"What's going on, Parker?"

"Did you read that?" She pointed toward the kitchen as if they could see the paper through the walls of her room.

"I did."

"And?"

"And what? Why are you so upset?"

"My question to you, Mickey Finn, is why aren't YOU upset?"

"I don't pay attention to those stories, Parker. They don't mean anything. What she wrote about happened before we met," he said soothingly.

"Poor you, Mickey, you didn't know about the revolving door to my bedroom."

"That doesn't mean anything to me. Should we talk about the revolving door to *my* bedroom?" He tried a small smile, hoping to calm her down. "You weren't the only one named in that article."

"Oh, well, that makes it all better than. I almost can't hear you over the ticking stop watch." She glared at him. "What are we doing anyway? What the fuck is this?"

Mickey startled at the question.

"Yeah, you don't have a clue do you, Rod?"

She pushed past him and out the door. Tony was already waiting for her. She quickly climbed into the backseat and asked him to take her to the studio. She pulled out her phone and texted Brynn.

Parker: *You up?*

Brynn: *For a couple hours already. What's up?*

Parker: *Feel like company?*

Brynn: *Sure.*

Parker: *See you soon.*

"Change of plans Tony, can we go to the Oxford Hotel please."

"Sure thing Ms. Parker."

Parker slumped against the back seat of the car. Her mother would have been proud of that award-winning performance. Sure. she was angry, wishing nothing but the worst for Lucinda, but that story couldn't have been published at a better time.

This was her exit strategy. She could have easily allowed Mickey to calm her down. When he had confronted her so calmly in her room, she knew that he was not upset about her life, that he probably already knew all about it. Besides, he could hardly fault her for her romantic track record when his was just as bad, if not worse.

Yeah, this was what was needed to put some distance between her and Mickey. Why didn't she feel better about it?

She always knew, without question, that her dad loved her mother. From since she could remember, she noticed how he always went out of his way to make his mother happy. He was one of the best cooks in L.A., people flocked to his restaurant, the waiting list was months long, yet they always went out for dinner, his mother dressed to the nines, his father happy to have her on his arm. He catered to her at home, making her coffee, giving her flowers, sweets, and jewelry.

It wasn't until she was in her mid-teens that she saw for the first time that her mother was a master manipulator when it came to her dad. How she would withhold her affection from him when she was not happy. At first, she thought it was only her imagination, but when Parker began to get calls from boys, her mother began to give her hints on how to "handle" them.

"Parker, such a cute teddy bear from that boy," her mother fawned over the tiny stuffie she received from her then boyfriend, "but so small. Tell him that next time. Don't be satisfied with the small things, always aim for bigger and better."

"Parker, does that boy deserve your best kisses?" she would ask. "Don't give him your best until he gives you his best. He must work to make you happy."

She began to notice that, although her father would give her mother beautiful bouquets of flowers, her mother would say something like "No red roses to show your love" or "No lilies for easter", always something to make him try harder and still show him that his best efforts were not enough.

"Parker, this is my most important lesson. Your body is the greatest reward for good behavior. When a man does what he should do to make you happy, that is when you share yourself, that is when you maybe do something special that you would not normally do for your man."

From that day onward she could tell when her dad had

done his best to make her mother happy. When he started his day happy, with smiles at the breakfast table, he had made her mother happy and her mother had expressed her appreciation the night before.

No wonder she was so screwed up. She absolutely rejected her mother's advice. She saw that her mother's system was successful in that it brought her dad to heel, but, in the end, nothing was ever good enough for her mother who, for a woman who should have been happy at being pampered and adored by her husband, was a bitter shrew who constantly demanded more. Parker did not understand how her father could still love such a manipulative woman. Was he so blind to the way he was being played by her?

All she knew was that she chose happiness. She made her own money and it was good. She could buy herself the biggest and the best, if she so chose. She didn't have to manipulate some man into giving it to her. Why her relationships never lasted for more than a week at most had nothing to do with what he could give her. They were fun but there was no substance there and that was another big problem all of a sudden. Fucking Mickey Finn had substance.

$$\$\$\$$$

"So, how're things with the billionaire?" Brynn asked as she pulled a blouse off the rack and held it up to look at it before putting it back.

Parker was a short rack ahead of Brynn. "Okay, I guess," she responded,

"You guess? You're the only one who would know, except for Mickey, of course."

"They're good. He's great, really," she responded. Why did she suddenly feel like crying? Crying! She never cried, not over some guy anyway! She took a deep breath in before slowly exhaling.

"Maybe not so great?" Brynn hinted.

Parker looked up at her, tears forming in her eyes.

"Let's go get a drink," Brynn said as she hooked her arm in Parker's.

$$$

"He is great, Brynn, that's the big problem," Parker said staring into her drink.

Her phone dinged. She took it out of her purse and saw the text from Mickey: *Feeling better, baby?*

"See?" She showed the text to Brynn. "He's checking up on me. How considerate is that?" She returned her phone to her purse without replying.

"Exactly why is that a problem?" Brynn asked.

"What's going to happen with us?" Parker asked. "I can tell you how this is going to go, two possible outcomes. One, neither of us have any real experience with relationships so either one of us is going to lose interest in the very near future; or, two, if, by some miracle we can have a committed relationship, we live in different cities on different ends of the country and long-distance relationships are almost guaranteed to fail. Either way, it's going to end."

"That's a pretty fatalistic view. You've ended this before you've even given it a chance to develop. Are you telling me this is your plan? This is where you want it to go from here?"

"Yeah. I'm just trying to minimize damage to me, and to him. If I left today it would hurt. If I leave next week, it would be worse and if I leave in another two weeks or a month it would be unbearable."

"Sounds to me like you've found something good and you're scared," Brynn said.

"He doesn't do girlfriends or dating or relationships. But then again, neither do I."

"Maybe you've both been looking for each other. Why not stick around and see what happens?"

"Oh my God, Brynn, are you a closet romantic? Tell me it's not true!"

"You know, Parker, you've had more dick than most girls I know. You must have had at least one of every kind. What more are you looking for? Maybe that's what you should be asking yourself."

"Fuck, I hate you sometimes, Brynn," she said. Maybe that was what she should be asking herself.

$$$

It was late, she and Brynn had had dinner, gone to see a movie, and were back in Brynn's suite for more drinks.

Parker's phone dinged again. It was Mickey, again: *Where are you?* This was his fourth message today, none of which she had responded to. Time to turn the screw, she thought to herself.

Parker: *Out. Staying over at a friend's.*
He responded immediately.
Mickey: *What friend?*
She looked at his text before turning off her phone.

CHAPTER 15
Mickey

It was the fourth night since he had last seen Parker. She refused to respond to his texts. He didn't see her on Monday night or Tuesday night either. She came home late both nights, after he was asleep. The only way he knew she was home was that he saw her shoes at the door and her purse in the living room. She had stopped using Tony to drive her so he couldn't even ask Tony where she was.

He had no idea what was happening, why she had distanced herself from him, why she stopped communicating with him. He kept rethinking their last night together, wondering if he had said or done something wrong but, no, she had been happy when they came home. They had had a great night.

Was it something he had done on Sunday morning? They were all good when he left the bed, but she had been in a foul mood from the moment she came into the living area and Lucinda's article seemed to push her over the edge.

What he did know was that, on Sunday, Tony had dropped her off at the Oxford Hotel. Who did she know that was staying at a hotel? Was that where she spent the night? Which led to the next question: was she sleeping with someone else?

He was frustrated and angry. He couldn't focus at work. She was messing with his head. He tried to text her one last time:

Mickey: *What is going on Parker? We need to talk. Can you come home early today?*

He wasn't surprised when she didn't respond. He had sent her that text five hours ago. He was torn between staying at work to start working on something else or going home to wait for her when his phone rang. It was her.

"Parker. Are you okay?"

"No, it's Brynn Williams, a friend of Parker's."

"Yes, Parker has spoken of you. Is she okay?"

"She is more than okay, Mickey, but I think you should come and get her."

"Sorry?"

"We're at the studio. Your man, Tony, knows where it is. She's fine but she's going to need some help. You should come to get her."

"Okay. I'll be there as soon as I can."

"Good. I look forward to meeting you."

Mickey ended the call and then called Tony immediately. He put his jacket on, made sure he had his wallet and keys and then took the elevator down to the car, which was already at the curb, waiting for him.

He was at the studio in half an hour. He entered the building. It was quiet, the décor subdued. He walked down the hall, following the music and then the odor of marijuana wafting toward him. He entered the sound booth, his path blocked by a tall, thin Rasta, inhaling a huge joint. He eyed Mickey, blew out a lungful of aromatic smoke before speaking in a heavy accent.

"You da brudder sister Brynn call?"

A blonde appeared at the fellow's side. "You're Mickey," she said as she held out her hand. "Brynn Williams."

He took her hand and shook it.

"This is Saint," she said referring to the tall Rasta. "He and his crew dropped in out of nowhere today. We weren't expecting him." She glared at Saint.

Saint took her in his arms and hugged her. "Blessings, baby."

Brynn shrugged out of his arms and looked at Mickey. "She's over here," she said, turning away from him.

Parker was on a couch, squished between four other Rastas. She looked at Brynn, her gaze then travelling to Mickey. Her eyes were wide and red. A happy smile spread across her face, her eyes crinkling at the corners.

"Mickey Finn," she said on a breath, like she couldn't believe her eyes.

All the stress flew out of his body at the way she looked at him. He could tell she was happy and relieved to see him. He crouched on the floor in front of her, meeting her eyes.

"Hey, baby," he greeted her.

"Mickey Finn," she repeated.

"The one and only." He smiled at her.

She held out her hand. He took it, stood, and pulled her up into his arms. She wrapped her arms around him, her cheek on his chest. She released him and turned to Brynn. "See, Brynn," she said, "see."

Brynn laughed at her. "I see, Parker." She looked at Mickey. "Thanks for coming to get her, Mickey."

Saint put his hand on Parker's shoulder. "Little sister, she's not good with the ganja." He chuckled.

"Yeah, not the industrial strength, Saint," Brynn chastised him.

Mickey couldn't quite figure out the dynamic between them. Saint seemed to dote on Brynn. She just seemed to be annoyed by him. It suddenly occurred to him that he had heard of Saint. Even though he didn't listen to Reggae music or know much about the culture, Saint was so well known that you just knew his name.

"You wanna go home, baby?" Mickey asked Parker.

Parker nodded her head yes. Mickey found her coat, helped her put it on, and picked up her purse. With his arm around her shoulder, he guided her out of the studio and into the car.

They rode in silence, holding hands. Parker lifted her hand to her face. It was Mickey's hand that touched her. She gasped and then rubbed his hand against her face again. She gripped his hand tighter and whined.

Mickey looked over at her, surprised at the look of panic on her face. "What's wrong, Parker?" he asked.

"I can't feel my face." She dabbed at her face with his hand. "Mickey, do I still have a face?"

He smiled at her. "Yes, and it's beautiful, baby." He pulled her onto his lap putting his arms around her. "I've got you, Parker. There's nothing to be afraid of."

She settled against him, listening to the steady beat of his heart which calmed her down. When they got home, Mickey took her coat off and hung it up. He took her hand and sat her at the kitchen island.

"Are you hungry? Thirsty?"

"Do you have any cake?" she whispered.

"Sorry, no, not today."

"Cookies? Chips? Ice cream? Anything snacky?"

"I can make you some toast and jam. That's as snacky as I have."

"Okay."

He made her two pieces of toast with strawberry jam. He slid the plate across the island to her. She inhaled them and looked at him.

"Would you like more?"

"Yes, please."

He made her another two pieces of toast and jam. He also gave her a glass of milk. She ate the toast, drank the milk and dragged the back of her hand over her mouth when she was finished. She slipped off the stool and walked to her room.

Mickey, cleaned up the kitchen, then walked down the hall. The door to her room was closed. He was going to knock, then thought better of it. He didn't think Parker was in any condition for a discussion. He sighed and continued down the hall to his room. He undressed, brushed his teeth, and came back to find Parker in his bed.

He slid under the covers, thinking she was asleep. She slid across the sheets and wrapped herself around him, her leg over his, her arm across his chest. She lifted her head and kissed his jaw.

"I missed you, Rod," she whispered as her hand slid down his chest to his boxers.

He put his hand over hers. "I don't know if this is a good idea, baby, you are really wasted," he said.

"This is always a good idea," she said as she slid her hand under his boxers. "Umm hmmm," she murmured as she fondled him.

Mickey moaned. She straddled him, leaning down to grind her lips into his, demanding a response to her desire. He was hard in seconds, pushing against his boxers, requesting release. Parker leaned over him, pulled a condom out of his night stand and slid off him. She pulled down his boxers, releasing his cock. Her hands held the condom wrapper, ready to rip it open. At the sight of his erect cock, she dropped the package, gripped his cock, bent toward it and slid her tongue over the head.

"Baby," he ground out, "are you sure?"

She didn't respond, instead, taking all of him into her mouth at once. Furiously, she slid him in and out of her mouth, her other hand massaging his balls. He watched as she took all of him in his mouth.

"Fuck," he swore as he pulled out of her mouth, found the condom package, ripped it open, slid it on, and threw her on the bed. She looked up at him with lust in her eyes, her legs splayed, waiting for him. He plunged into her and stayed there, savoring the feel that he had been craving for the past three days. She was so wet, he slid in and out of her with ease. She met each of his thrusts, her legs wrapped around his waist, urging him on. He reached for one of her breasts, twisting a nipple as he pumped in and out of her. She put her hand on top of his. She was moaning as he rode her. She watched his face, her orgasm beginning to build in her. She saw his jaw tighten, the veins in his neck pulse and knew that he was going to come any second.

He gritted his teeth. "Come for me baby," he said as he pushed into her. "This cock has missed you."

He pinched her nipple one more time and she came with a scream. He continued to pound into her, seeking his release. "You're mine, baby. Mine," he shouted as he came deep within her. He held her down on the bed as he emptied his seed in her, jerking with every spurt.

Exhausted, he pulled out of her. He lay on his back. Being inside her, seeing her, had been like coming home. He had missed her. He closed his eyes and wondered if she was here to stay. Why wouldn't she? She had been so happy to see him, so anxious to have him, so responsive to his touch.

He rolled out of bed and went into the bathroom to discard the condom and clean himself off. When he slid back into bed Parker wrapped herself around him, her arm across his chest, her leg pushing between his. Her head was on his shoulder. She rubbed her face against him, sighing contentedly. She was asleep seconds later.

$$$

She was still wrapped around him when he woke the next morning, as if neither of them had moved all night. He was overcome with a sense of comfort, as if all was right with the world. He rubbed her back, loving the feel of her body on his.

She stirred and rolled off him, opening her eyes. She turned her head and met his eyes, a look of concern crossing her features.

"Morning, baby," he said, his voice gruff.

She grunted at him and slid out of bed, running into his bathroom. She was back after answering the call of nature. She slid under the covers, pushed herself back over to him and repositioned herself. She was asleep again within moments. Mickey picked his phone up from the nightstand and began to go through his emails. He emailed his assistant telling her to rearrange his schedule. He wasn't going in to work this morning.

$$$

He woke up as Parker was leaving his room. He smiled as he watched her cute ass as it disappeared out his door before sliding out of bed and putting on his boxers. He got out of bed and went to find her.

She was next door in her room getting dressed. She looked up at him when he entered.

"I'm late, Mickey. You should have woken me up. I have to go," she said.

"I thought we could spend the morning together, Parker."

"I can't Mickey. I have a job. I can't... Shit, where is my purse?"

"It's in the living room." He moved out of the way and followed behind her. He was annoyed. "We need to talk, Parker."

"I know," she said, "I know, but I have to go. Can Tony give me a ride to the studio or do you need him right away?" She was texting, not looking at him.

"Tony can drive you. Parker, look at me," he demanded.

She finished typing and sent her text, before meeting his eyes. "What?"

"I need to speak to you, Parker. Can you come home after the studio tonight? We can have dinner and talk."

She smiled at him. "Sure," she said before running out the door.

$$$

She didn't come home at all that night, or the night after that. She did not respond to his texts and did not answer his calls.

CHAPTER 16
Parker

She was so angry at herself. She was also annoyed at Brynn for calling Mickey last night.

Yesterday, they had been on the third attempt at getting down a track when Pax suddenly stopped singing. She continued drumming, keeping the beat. She looked over at Keith and Trent and then they stopped playing guitar, staring into the control booth. She stopped drumming and looked into the booth to see what everyone was looking at.

Saint was in the booth—his arms around Brynn, who looked royally pissed—along with the other six members of his posse and two bodyguards. She smirked. She was not surprised that Saint showed up. He tried to be wherever Brynn was.

Pax turned to her. "Is that…"

"Yes," she responded. "None other than Saint." She stood, put her sticks down, and walked into the booth.

"Saint," she greeted him.

"Little Parker," he smiled as he enveloped her in a hug. He was a big hugger. He released her and she went down the line, greeting his posse and bodyguards, all of whom she knew.

That was the end of work that day. If Saint was breathing, he was toking. Joints were in constant rotation. Brynn sat at the control board with Saint, playing the tracks that they had been working on for the past month. Parker sat with the band and Saint's posse, toking, drinking, sharing stories. It had been at least six months since she had seen them all.

Food had been delivered and the party just kept on going. Time slipped away. Parker could toke with the best of them but toking with Saint and his posse was on a whole other level. She had lost track of time and was having difficulty following any conversation when she looked up to see Mickey.

When he met her eyes, she felt as though her heart would explode. She was so happy to see him, so relieved that he was there for her.

And then she woke up this morning, wrapped in Mickey, surrounded by his smell, his weight and comfort. All the effort she had put into avoiding him and distancing herself from him in the last few days was all shot to shit.

She had wanted to stay in bed with him but she really was late for work. She wanted to stop and enjoy a few moments with him before she ran out of the house but she wouldn't allow herself that luxury. He was annoyed at her. He understood that she had to go to work but he wanted to talk to her. She could have easily taken care of that, a few soft words, a hug, maybe a few kisses to allay his fears, but she wouldn't.

She promised him that she would be home that night to have dinner with him and talk, but she knew as soon as she agreed to it that she wouldn't be there. She had to get out of there, she had to get away from him.

The next day she had stormed into the studio. When Brynn greeted her, she glared at her, walked past her and into the studio. She threw her coat on the floor, sat behind her kit and started whaling on her drums. She played *Wipeout* five times in a row. When she was done, she was wet with sweat, she stood and hurled her drumstick at the thick glass of the booth, right at Brynn's face. She followed with her other drumstick.

"You shouldn't have called him, Brynn," she said, glaring at her through the glass.

Brynn leaned toward a microphone, pushed a button and said, "I'm sorry, Parker, really."

They looked at each other for a tense moment. Parker nodded her head and Brynn sent the band into the studio. Time to get to work.

Work on the album was progressing. Brynn thought they would be done in another week or two. They worked all day, then Saint and his crew would show up and the rest of the evening was just hanging around, talking, drinking, toking.

Parker would allow herself a few minutes each day to think about Mickey. She would pull out her phone and look at his texts, which had stopped all together. She would pull up the few photos she had of him before closing the gallery app, taking a deep breath and rejoining the party.

Again, she was arranging her own transportation to and

from the house. She only came home when she was certain that Mickey would be sleeping. She would sleep until after he left for work. It all worked like clockwork for another week.

They had finished work for the day, they were all hanging around in the booth and the studio. Suddenly, there was another commotion in the booth. Colin Columbo and his body guards were there.

"Hey, Brynn," he called to Brynn. "Heard you were in town. I'm at the arena tomorrow night, thought I would pop in to say hi."

"Colin," Brynn hugged him, "great to see you. Do you know Saint?"

Introductions were made, Saint passed Colin a joint, Colin pulled in a lungful and, scanning the room, stopped on Parker.

"Is that Parker?" he asked.

"Hey, Colin," Parker said.

Colin Columbo—the panty whisperer—and Parker Chen had a past. They had been a thing for a very short time but remained friends with benefits. Colin was a top ten singer/songwriter known for his make-out music, hence the panty whisperer nickname. The man was a looker and had a way with women as well. His nickname was well earned.

Colin came up to her, wrapped her in a hug and kissed her on the lips. He leaned in and whispered in her ear, "Good to see you, Parker. I've missed you."

She laughed at him. "I'm sure you have, Colin." Colin may be missing many things, but female companionship was not one of them.

He released her but slid his hand down her back and rested it on her ass. "You still look so tasty girl." He leaned forward and kissed her neck. "What are you doing after?" he asked.

"Yes, Parker, what are you doing after?" a voice asked behind her.

She knew, before she even turned around, who it was. She stepped away from Colin, pushing his hand off her ass, before turning to Mickey. Mickey...who was glaring at her.

"No plans, yet," she said, meeting his eyes.

"Hey, man, Colin Columbo," Colin said as he stuck his hand out to Mickey.

Mickey ignored him, staring at Parker. She read the anger in his eyes. She knew what he was thinking but she didn't deny it. Instead, she raised her chin in defiance, not offering an explanation or any comforting words.

Mickey simply turned and left without another word.

"Who was that guy?" Colin asked behind her.

"That was Mickey Finn," she replied.

"Who the fuck is Mickey Finn? He seems like a real dick."

"No, he's not. He's a really great guy. He's actually wonderful."

"Better than me?" Colin teased as he put his arm around her again. "Tell the truth, Parker."

A thousand times better, she thought to herself. "As if that's possible, Colin," she said.

$$$

Tony picked her up two hours later. She slid into the car. "Is he at home?" she asked.

"No, Ms. Parker, he's still at the office."

"Can you take me to him, please, Tony?"

"Yes, Ms. Parker."

Fifteen minutes later, Tony pulled up to Mickey's building. He opened the door for Parker and took her into the foyer. He nodded at the security guard and pushed the elevator button. They rode in silence to the twentieth floor. Tony swiped a card to open the door to Renewal Developments and led her through the dark office to a set of double doors.

"His office, Ms. Parker. I'll be in the car."

"Thank you, Tony."

She turned the knob and entered his office. Mickey was sitting in the dark, a glass of scotch in his hand, looking out at the city lit up below him.

She approached him. She sat on his lap, took the glass out of his hand and took a sip of the scotch, before giving it back to him. "I'm not sorry," she whispered.

He put the glass on the end table and looked up at her. He slid his knuckles down her cheek, down her neck, to the knot closing her coat. He undid it and opened her coat. She was wearing a yellow bikini.

He lightly ran his fingers from her neck down between her breasts. Nonchalantly, he unclasped her bra, pushing the fabric off her breasts.

"You have such perfect tits," he said as he cupped one of them. "They fit my hand and my mouth perfectly." He leaned forward and sucked her nipple into his mouth. He circled her nipple with his tongue. She arched her back, pushing her breasts closer to him.

He released her nipple and then trailed his hand from her breast down her stomach. Her abs contracted at his touch. Leisurely he ran his finger under the top hem of her bikini bottoms. His hand fell to her side, untying the bow that was there. He pushed the material aside.

He slid a finger through her folds. She opened her legs. He slowly rubbed her clit. "I thought we agreed this was mine," he said. "But someone else has been here, haven't they?"

"No, Mickey, no one." She gasped as she tried to push against his hand but his arm around her waist prevented her from moving.

His fingers came back to her face. He traced her lips with his fingers. "You have a beautiful mouth," he said, as he slipped a finger between her lips. He pulled her face down to his and lightly brushed his lips over hers. "Such a pretty mouth and nothing but lies come out."

He met her eyes.

"No, Mickey."

"Yes, baby, lies. Where have you been?"

"I've been working."

"And what else?"

"Hanging out with my friends."

"Why haven't you been at the house? In my bed?"

She couldn't look at him anymore. She turned her head away from his gaze.

"Whatever this was," he grabbed her chin and forced

her to look at him, "it's over. I don't play these games, baby. You know that."

He pushed her off his lap and stood. "You should leave now. Tony will take you wherever you want to go."

Parker pulled her clothes together. She tugged the belt of her coat closed and left his office without a word. That hurt. This was what she wanted though, wasn't it? If this is what she wanted, why did it hurt so much?

CHAPTER 17
Parker

Two weeks later, her work on the album was done. She and Brynn were going to catch a morning flight back to L.A. on Saint's jet. It was an early evening for her but she had things she had to do.

She got out of her uber and entered the house. The lights were on and there was some faint music playing. She slipped out of her shoes and walked into the living area, putting her purse on the table where she usually did.

She heard Mickey talking and hesitated. He came out of the hallway leading to the bedrooms, a tall, slim blonde was behind him, giggling at something he said. Parker froze.

He was looking behind himself saying something to the blonde. When he turned, he met her eyes and stopped. He put his arm around the blonde and steered her to the other side of himself, farther away from Parker. Their eyes locked, neither saying anything.

"Hello," the blonde broke the tension, "I'm Sherilynn Morrow. Mickey, where are your manners?" She hit him on the chest. "Who is your cute little friend?"

Mickey turned to Sherilynn, his voice low and charming. "She's not my friend," he said as he met Parker's eyes. "She knows Toby. This is Parker Chen. She's been working in the city for the past month or so. She's been staying here."

"Doing what?" Sherilynn looked at Parker.

"Just…" she hesitated looking briefly at Mickey. "Just some music work, nothing too exciting."

"Sounds interesting," Sherilynn said. "Why don't you join us? We were just going to have some cake and coffee."

Parker's eyes shot to Mickey's again. He raised his eyebrows at her. Smiling, she looked back at Sherilynn. "No, thank you. I've had a long day. I'm just going to take a bath and get some sleep. It was a pleasure to have met you."

"You too, Parker," she said, all sweetness and light. She put her hand on Mickey's arm. "You said cheesecake, right? I love cheesecake."

Parker hurried down the hall to her room, closing and locking the door behind her. This was great. This was what she wanted, right? She jammed her fist into her mouth, stifling the sob that came out of her mouth. Mickey certainly didn't waste any time, did he?

She stripped off her clothes and ran a bath. She sank into the hot water. Did she just hear Mickey laugh? She slid deeper into the tub, letting the water cover her ears.

$$$

Her alarm went off ten minutes after Mickey always left for work. She had packed last night. Everything was ready for her to go. She quickly walked into the living area to confirm that he had gone to work. She walked back down the hall, into Mickey's bedroom. She went into his closet, found her favorite cologne, sprayed some on herself and came back into the bedroom. That was the only thing of his that she was taking with her. She stopped to look at the bed, then turned and went into her room.

She came out pulling her suitcase behind her. She grabbed her purse, slung it over her shoulder, slid on her shoes and got into the uber waiting for her on the corner. She didn't look back but she pulled a pair of sunglasses out of her purse and put them on. She wouldn't take them off until she was in her house in L.A., the only thing remaining of Mickey Finn was the scent that she wore and that would wear off as the hours passed.

$$$

Mickey

The house was quiet and dark when he got home that night. He assumed Parker was not home. He also assumed he wouldn't be seeing much of her anymore. Not after last night. He knew that she was hurt and it killed him that he was the cause, but he had to move on, he had to let her go.

It was ironic that she was the one that had lost interest in him, funny almost. There had been almost anything he would have done to make her happy, to keep her with him, anything but that. He would not be played a fool. He would not wait in the wings for her crumbs of attention while she amused herself with someone else.

He walked down the hall to his room. He turned on the light and stopped, looking at his bed. Neatly laid out at the foot of his bed were her garment bag, the black velvet jewelry box and his T-shirt.

He spun and stormed into the guest room. Everything was neat and tidy. He opened the dresser drawers—empty. He looked in the closet—nothing but hangers.

Where the fuck was she?

He called Tony and went directly to the studio. He walked down the hall to the control booth he had found her in before. There was one guy with headphones on sitting at the board, adjusting sliders. He saw Mickey and took his headphones off.

"Where is everyone?" Mickey asked.

"Oh," he replied. "They're done. I think Brynn flew back to L.A. with Saint and Parker this morning. Do you need to get in touch with someone?"

"No. Thanks," he said as he left the studio, a huge hole in his heart.

CHAPTER 18
Mickey

Six months later Mickey's Village project was under way. Ground had been broken and a foundation was being poured. He was looking at another property on the east side of the city, deciding how best to develop the area.

He rarely thought of Parker now. Only once an hour. He had just completed the one minute per hour he allocated to thoughts of her and forced himself to look down at his phone, checking his calendar. He was meeting his friends at his club in half an hour. That should just give him enough time to call his contractor to discuss the Village project.

$$\$\$\$$$

He entered the bar at the club and found Paul, Sven, and Darshan sitting at a table, waiting for him. He placed his order and caught up with the guys before they headed into the dining room for dinner. They talked briefly about the Village project before moving onto other topics.

They were enjoying an aperitif when Darshan asked about her.

"Mickey, you still seeing Parker? I haven't seen her since I went to the studio. I thought for sure you would have brought her."

"Parker is back in L.A.," he told Darshan. "She left about six months ago."

"You two still in touch?" he asked.

"Definitely not, Darshan," he responded curtly, attempting to end this line of discussion.

Darshan heard the tone in his voice, knowing not to ask any further questions, allowing a change of topic from Sven.

$$$

Mickey was reviewing some of the due diligence reports on the property in the east when his assistant buzzed him. He pushed the button on his head set. "What?" he barked.

"I have Brynn Williams on the line. She's actually called a number of times, but never left a message. Says she knows you. Do you want me to transfer the call?"

Mickey sat back in his chair. "Sure, put her through."

He heard the call click over. "Brynn, it's been a while."

"Mickey, I want you to acknowledge how hard it is to get in touch with you," she said.

"Acknowledged." He chuckled. "What can I do for you, Brynn?" he asked.

"I see that your brother's band has been nominated for a Grammy. Just wondering if you've been in touch with him about that."

"Yes, I have. I'm very proud of him and his band. The

guys have certainly worked hard and long enough to finally get the recognition."

"Will they be at the ceremony? Do you know?"

"Yes, they will be there. Did you want to get in touch with them?" He had no idea where this conversation was leading. He wanted to be done with it. "Although, I have to say I don't know what the band's plans are. Do you want an introduction?"

"What? An introduction for what? Oh, an introduction for me. Mickey, I have enough people coming to me for my services, I certainly don't need to be soliciting new clients." she laughed.

"I don't want to be rude, Brynn, but I do have work to do. What can I do for you?"

"Okay, just wondering if you were going to be at the ceremony with them."

"Not sure about that, Brynn. Why do you ask?"

"I'll be there," she said. "I'm bringing Parker with me."

She was greeted with silence. Finally, Mickey spoke. "I don't know what Parker told you about us, Brynn, but she definitely is not interested in seeing me again. I don't chase after women who have no interest in me."

"You know, it's not an excuse, Mickey, it is an explanation," Brynn said, "but her mother really fucked with her head growing up. Parker has changed since you. She is a different person. If you think she's not interested in you, that she's not hurting because she isn't seeing you, you are wrong. If you have any feelings for her, if you still haven't shut the door on her, well, I just wanted to present you with an opportunity, some insider information."

More silence on the line before he said, "I'll keep that in mind. Thanks for calling."

"Well, will I see you there?"

"No idea."

"I know what she did to you at the end, Mickey. I couldn't reason with her about it. But just so you know, those nights when she didn't go home, she was in my suite on the couch. She didn't cheat on you while she was there. She never said anything negative about you, ever."

"Thank you for that, Brynn," he said sincerely.

"She still hasn't been with anyone since she got home Mickey and that's not what she was like. She has really changed."

"As I said, Brynn, I have work to do."

"So, no commitment on the ceremony then?"

"No. It's been a pleasure to speak with you again, but I have a meeting I need to get to."

"Okay, then. Maybe I'll see you soon."

"Goodbye," he said before he hung up.

CHAPTER 19
Parker

Her hair was longer now. She had bangs that stopped just above her eyebrows. Her straight, blunt-cut hair was pulled back into a ponytail that ended just below her neck. She wore a black fedora pulled low onto her forehead.

She stood beside Brynn on the red carpet, in a black double-breasted pin-striped suit, her red lace bra the only thing under her jacket. Her black Manolo boots gave her an extra two inches. They stopped and posed for the photographers. She put her hands into the pocket of her wide-leg pants, standing sideways beside Brynn.

Brynn smiled at the cameras, her breasts pushed up ridiculously high in a black leather bustier over short black leather shorts and knee-high black boots.

"I look like a fucking dominatrix or something," Brynn said to Parker between her clenched teeth. "All I need is a riding crop."

Parker laughed. "You look stunning, bitch. My feet are killing me in these boots."

"Try beathing with your tits under your neck in a bustier it took two burly men to tie."

"Just two," she teased her friend. "I hope we're not spending any length of time on our feet. I need to sit down."

"Soon enough," Brynn said as she put her arm around Parker's waist and repositioned her, looking toward the right for another barrage of camera flashes.

They took a few steps further down the carpet when they were suddenly pulled backward into a hug, the smell of marijuana enveloping them.

"Saint," Brynn exclaimed. She shook herself, trying to get out of his grip.

"You know I was coming to dis," he said as he smiled at the cameras, Brynn and Parker on each side of him, his posse standing behind them.

They walked the carpet slowly with Saint and his crew. It was the biggest award ceremony of the year. People they hadn't seen for years were in attendance. It was like homecoming, running into a different friend they hadn't seen for a while with almost every step they took.

They finally made it into the venue. Brynn and Saint went to the bar. Parker went to the ladies' room to sit down for a few minutes and refresh her make up.

Parker was enjoying herself. This was the first time in six months, since Mickey, that she had gone anywhere besides the studio, the grocery store, and her house. When she wasn't working, she was practicing, the soundtracks she drummed to drowning out her thoughts of Mickey. She had lost weight, her muscles more toned than they were before. She wasn't sleeping that well anymore either. She dreamed of Mickey, sometimes just his blue eyes looking at her with lust and the sound of his deep voice, waking her up to the disappointment that he wasn't there.

She was also pretty sure that he hated her for what she had done. He had accused her of cheating on him, of lying to him, and she hadn't but he didn't believe her. She still couldn't think of being with another man. She was even turning down her friends with benefits that she used to dally with.

Brynn had finally forced her to come to this event, and she was glad to be here, among old friends, dressed to slay, and ready to party. Time to move on, she hoped. She had to put Mickey behind her once and for all or she was going to start buying cats and become a crazy cat lady. She knew she had it in her to do that.

She came back into the lobby and ran into Temptation.

"Hey, Parker," Toby Finn called out to her. LeShawn and Marcus turned in her direction.

She gasped when she saw him. Until this very moment she hadn't realized how much he and Mickey looked alike. She pasted on a smile and walked toward them, greeting them with hugs.

"Congrats on the nomination, guys," she said.

"You going to the afterparty, Parker?" LeShawn asked.

"You think I got dressed up just to sit in an audience for three hours," she chided him. "I'll be there."

"Yeah? Let's hook up then. It's been a while," Toby said.

"Drinks on you, Toby."

"It's a deal," he said as he winked and walked away.

Not for the first, the tenth, or the fiftieth time that day, she thought of Mickey. She knew that she had hurt him but, what surprised her was that she had hurt herself just as badly, if not more. She missed him every minute of every day. In the mornings she thought of him with his coffee and the paper and no shirt. In the afternoon she thought of him at the farmers market with her. In the evenings, well, she thought a lot of different things about him and he was always naked.

She had never had sex like that with anyone before him and, truthfully, she was not interested in sex with anyone else since him and she had received offers. Sometimes she thought maybe he had ruined her for every other man, but then she would tell herself it would just take time to get over him. But it was already six months. How much longer would be reasonable? Like, come on, it's not like they had been married or even in a long-term relationship.

The gong indicating fifteen minutes to curtain rang through the lobby.

Thank Christ, she was going to be able to sit down.

$$$

The show ran over, as it always did. What kept it interesting was seeing all the people she knew hosting, presenting, performing, and winning awards.

Brynn won for producing Saint's last album, her fourth Grammy. Her speech was short and funny.

Temptation won for single of the year. Their name was called and the camera flashed to them in the crowd. Parker watched their surprise and happiness on the giant screen over the stage. They stood, laughing and hugging their guests and wives.

The camera pulled back and a face flashed on the screen, Parker whipped her head behind her to see where Temptation was seated. She could have sworn she saw Sherilynn Morrow at the end of Temptation's seats, clapping for their win, but Parker couldn't see their row from where she sat. Her eyes returned to the stage.

Toby gave the acceptance speech, happy, thanking everyone they had ever met in their entire lives. Moments later the orchestra started up, drowning him out and playing the band off the stage.

$$$

At last, the ceremony was over. She was at the afterparty with Brynn. They were seated along the wall in a semi-circular banquette. Music was blaring, drinks were flowing, and friends and associates were moving from one table to the other, chatting for a bit before moving on to the next table.

Parker was speaking to Brynn when someone slid into the banquette behind her.

"I told you I was buying," a voice spoke from behind her. She turned and found Toby Finn sitting beside her with beers for her, Brynn, and him.

"Toby, congratulations on the win." She smiled at him.

"It was only a matter of time, Parker, you can't deny genius forever."

"Oh my God, there will be no living with you now!

You're going to have to walk sideways to get that huge ego through doorways."

"Parker Chen, right?"

Parker looked past Toby, meeting Sherilynn Morrow's eyes.

"I don't know if you remember me…"

"Sherilynn Morrow, yes. I remember you." She wanted to keep her voice civil and she thought she was doing a good job. It shouldn't matter to her that Sherilynn was with Mickey. But it did.

Toby looked from Sherilynn to Parker. "You know my sister? When did you meet?"

Parker looked at Toby. "Your sister? Sherilynn Morrow is your sister?"

Toby nodded.

Sherilynn said, "His married sister. Used to be Sherilynn Finn, Morrow now. We met at Mickey's place."

"I should have known," Toby said.

"Well, I just wanted to say hi, Parker," Sherilynn said. "I got the impression the last time we met wasn't a great time to be introduced."

"No," Parker denied, "it was all good, Sherilynn. Great to see you again."

"Parker Sexy Chen, how you doin'?"

Colin Columbo stopped beside Sherilynn. Parker rolled her eyes. "I should have known you were going to be here," she teased him. Parker watched as Sherilynn noticed Colin. She gasped and put her hand to her chest, then dropped it and twined it with her other hand.

"Colin, I want you to meet Sherilynn Morrow," Parker

said. Parker laughed when Colin looked at Sherilynn, took her hand in his, raised it to his lips and kissed her knuckles. Sherilynn almost fainted.

"Colin Columbo," she said. "I am a huge fan. I swear my oldest child was conceived to *Only You*."

"If I had a nickel for every time I heard something like that." Colin laughed.

"Let me guess, you'd have another million dollars," Parker shouted as the volume in the room increased.

Colin nodded and put his arm around Sherilynn's shoulder. "Let me buy you a drink, Sherilynn," he said as he led her away.

"There's Pretty Boys," Toby said to no one in particular. "I've gotta go say hi." He picked up his beer, clinked his bottle against Parker's before sliding out of the banquette and headed across the floor to the four-man band.

Parker turned back to speak to Brynn. Saint sat on the other side of her.

"I can't seem to dodge this guy," Brynn said into Parker's ear.

Someone else slid into the banquette behind Parker. Brynn's eyes briefly slid to whoever it was and nodded her head.

"I like him," Parker said to Brynn. An arm settled on the banquette behind her.

"I don't mind him," Brynn said, "but it's like he's stalking me. Every time I turn around, there he is. It's sort of creeping me out."

Parker leaned toward Brynn and said, in her best Saint impression, "It's all good, sister."

Brynn laughed. Saint said something in Brynn's ear. She nodded her head and they both slid out of the booth to hit the dance floor.

Parker sighed, took a sip of her beer, put it down on the table and looked over her shoulder to see what was happening in the room. She scanned the other banquettes beside theirs, the people on the floor and then went to the person sitting beside her. She spun around on the leather seat.

"Hi, baby," Mickey said, drinking her in with his eyes.

"Mickey Finn," she whispered.

"You look beautiful."

She was frozen, looking at his face, appreciating his arm across the back of the banquette, his chest taking up the space between the banquette and the table.

She had that feeling again, like her heart could explode. She was so happy to see him and he was sitting beside her, speaking to her. A tear slid out of her eye. She looked down, wiping it away with the back of her hand.

He reached forward and lifted her chin with his hand. "Are you all right, baby?" Concern filled his voice.

She met his eyes again. She opened her mouth. All that came out was "Mickey Finn."

"The one and only," he replied softly as he leaned forward and brushed his lips against hers. The room, the people, Brynn, and Saint all seemed to fade away. She was lost in his eyes.

CHAPTER 20
Mickey

"You don't like me anymore," she said, a hitch in her voice.

"Says who? You know you can't believe everything you read."

"You said so. You told your sister I wasn't your friend."

His brow furrowed. He knew he had said that. How to explain his way out of that one?

Since meeting her, it was like fate intervened every time there was a possibility that they would drift apart. First, Toby arranged for her to come back to the city for a layover. Then Brynn had called her out of the blue to arrange for her to work in the city for another six weeks. Then again, Brynn called him and told him that Parker would be at the Grammys.

He didn't believe in fate or luck or even coincidence, he was a self-made man. He made his own luck. Maybe this was him grasping at straws trying to get Parker back. This would be the last time though. He still wasn't willing to play any of her games, but he had to know if there was any chance for them to be together.

Another thing he didn't know was why he felt that his

life would be so much better with her in it. He could picture their daily life together and that was something he wanted. He just had to convince her that that was something she wanted as well.

"You combed your hair," he smiled, deflecting her last statement.

Parker's hand went to her ponytail. "Do you like it?" she asked.

"I like you," he replied, his eyes never leaving hers. Fuck, he wanted to grab her and kiss her.

"I like you too," she whispered as another tear slid down her cheek.

"Don't cry, baby," he said as he pulled her into his chest. This felt right, holding her here.

"It's a new thing," she said, pulling away. "I cry all the time now, at everything. You know that beer commercial with those horses—yeah, meltdown every time." She gave him a watery smile.

"Money! I didn't know you were here," Toby said from behind them.

Parker's eyes widened. Toby didn't know that Mickey was here?

Mickey turned toward Toby. "Yeah, I was going to call you. You know, bro, I love you, but I need you to fuck off right now. I'll talk to you tomorrow."

Toby wasn't expecting that reaction, Parker could tell by the shocked look on his face. His eyes slid to Parker, then back to Mickey. "Yeah, sure, bro. Whatever. Talk to you tomorrow."

Mickey turned back to Parker. "Why are you here, Mickey?" Parker asked.

"I'm here to see you," he replied. He watched her face as the words sunk in. "Do you want to go somewhere else? Somewhere more private so we can talk?"

"Uh." She hesitated for a moment before nodding her head.

Mickey slid out of the banquette and held out his hand to her. She took his hand and they left the party, Mickey holding her hand and leading her through the crowd, out of the building and into the parking lot. He flagged down one of the sedans working the event. "Where do you want to go?" he asked. "This is your town, baby. Do you want to go eat?"

She smiled up at him. "You know I could always go for cake."

He laughed and hugged her to his side. "Cake it is." They got in the sedan and Parker told the driver where to take them.

$$$

They were at a tiny table for two in a dimly-lit steakhouse. As soon as Parker had ordered the Billy Miner pie and put her hands on the table, Mickey took one in his, brought it to his lips, and kissed her knuckles. They sat in silence, staring into each other's eyes, until the waitress returned with the pie, which was actually a humongous piece of ice cream cake, and two forks.

"This is the best pie ever, Mickey," she said as she

picked up a fork and sliced off a piece of pie. She put it in her mouth, closed her eyes, and sighed.

He picked up his fork and took a slice of pie, maybe the only chance that he would get a taste of pie tonight. Parker was ruthless with a fork and a piece of cake.

"How's the Village project going?" she asked as she slid another piece of pie into her mouth.

"It's moving along," he replied. "The land has been cleared, we got our permits, and we are just about to start construction."

"And Potter's Creek?"

"A little delay there. the Community Committee has some concerns so we have to wait for city approval. Hey," he said as he watched her take another piece of pie, "are you keeping me talking so you can eat all the pie?"

She laughed, a small piece of ice cream, dribbled out of her mouth. She wiped it off with her napkin. "Am I that obvious?"

"Baby, when it comes to cake, it scares me to think of the things you would do to get it. But now that I'm on to you, what have you been doing?"

"Nothing much, just studio work."

"Who have you been working with?

"Colin Columbo recorded another album a couple of months ago. I was on that. Saint is working through a few things so when he's in the studio I'm with him and Brynn. I did some work on a movie sound track for a small independent film. Been thinking of buying some cats."

"Cats?"

"Yeah, thinking of maybe going into the crazy cat lady business. Haven't made a firm decision on that yet though."

"Good to know."

"I was really surprised to see you tonight, you know. I didn't think I would ever see you again and I wanted to tell you that I was sorry about how things turned out with us. I know it was my fault and—"

"I miss you, Parker," Mickey butted in. "I miss us. That's why I'm here. That's what I want to talk to you about."

Parker froze, a piece of pie balanced on her fork. Mickey was looking at her, watching her face, hoping for a response of some sort. "Uh," she said.

"I'm a man who goes after what he wants, Parker. The way things ended between us, I thought maybe we were done, that maybe you were done with me."

"No, Mickey, I…" She put down the fork. He was watching her, trying to figure out what she was thinking. Was she happy he was here? She looked down at the table and then looked away from him.

He reached over, putting his hand under her chin, redirecting her gaze to him. "I want you Parker," he said. "I want you in my bed when I wake up. I want you in my kitchen for coffee in the morning. I want you at home at the end of the day. I want you with me. All the time."

He had never put himself out like that for a woman but this felt so right. She felt so right. She had to say…anything. She was avoiding his eyes again.

"I…" She pulled in a deep breath, forcing herself to look at him. "I…" She looked away again.

God, she couldn't maintain eye contact with him. Had he just made a colossal mistake?

"I…" she whispered. Mickey leaned in to hear what she was saying. "I don't know if I can." She met his eyes. "I don't know if I can."

"What don't you know about, baby?" he asked.

"I've never had anybody stick with me," she said, looking down at the table. "I've never wanted to be with anyone for a long time."

"And?" he encouraged her to continue.

"And maybe I'm not meant to be with someone for a long time, maybe…"

Mickey, put his hand on her cheek and she leaned into it.

"Maybe I'm not a good person, Mickey." She placed her hand on top of his. "I don't want to hurt you."

"I'm willing to take that chance," he said.

"I don't want to be hurt either," she said, looking at him with tears in her eyes. "Last time really hurt, Mickey."

"Then don't leave this time, baby. Stay with me."

CHAPTER 21
Parker

He made it sound so easy—*Then don't leave. Stay with me*—was it that easy? Is that all she had to do? She wished it was. She hoped it was.

She twined her fingers with his and pulled his hand off her cheek. "Let's go," she said.

He paid the tab and they left the restaurant. The sedan was waiting for them. They got in the back and Parker gave the driver her address.

Mickey put his arm along the back of the seat. She snuggled up to him. He cupped her chin and raised her face to his. He bent down and gently kissed her. She leaned into him. He deepened the kiss, running his tongue along her bottom lip, teasing her mouth open. She opened her mouth under the onslaught of his lips.

Time sped by, it seemed like minutes before the sedan pulled up in front of her house and stopped. The driver discreetly coughed. Parker was partially straddling Mickey, his lips were on her neck, working his slow way back up to her lips. Her head was thrown back giving him access to her neck while she clung to him.

"We're here," the driver said.

Mickey pulled away from her neck, looking in her eyes before giving her a quick kiss on the lips. He pulled out his wallet, paid the driver and stepped out of the sedan. He put his hand out for Parker, helping her out of the car.

Walking in front of Mickey, Parker led him down the walk to her small bungalow. She opened the door allowing them access to the foyer. She quickly slipped off her shoes and proceeded down the short hallway into the living area, through to the kitchen.

"Do you want something to drink?" she asked.

He stood behind her. He put his hands on her shoulders. He leaned down. "No," he said into her neck before kissing her and slipping his tongue into her ear.

She moaned and leaned back into his chest. One of his hands slid down and undid the one button holding her jacket closed. Her jacket fell open revealing the red lace bra that she wore. His hand found her breast and gripped it while he continued to kiss her neck.

"Your tits are perfect," he said as his other hand found her other breast, gripping it. She arched her back, thrusting her breasts forward. His hands went to the front clasp of her bra and undid it. The cups of her bra fell forward leaving her breasts bare. His hands quickly found their way back to them, massaging them while he continued to kiss her neck, her chin, and her face.

Her hands fell to her waistband. She undid her pants and slid them down her hips to let them fall to the ground. She wore a matching red lace thong. Mickey ground his hips into her ass, letting her feel his erection, feel how hard he was for her. She pushed back against him.

"What, baby? What do you want?" His voice was deep and soft.

"You, Mickey. I want you in me, please," she said.

He released her breasts and stepped back. She turned to him, pulling her bra off her shoulders. He drank her in. Her hair was hanging around her face, her eyes were half open, her nipples were hard, he could see the wetness staining her thong.

She reached forward, grabbing his T-shirt, pulling it out of his pants and pushing it up his chest. He took over for her and pulled it over his head dropping it on the floor. She ogled his chest as her hands ran freely over him, his jaw clenched.

She dropped her hands, undid his belt, popped open the button of his jeans and slid down the zipper. His cock was there, waiting for her. She smiled as she slid the waistband of his briefs down over the head. She took him in her hand, running her thumb over the wet tip.

She lifted her thumb to her mouth and licked it. Mickey roared. He gripped her ass and set her on the counter. He pulled a small foil package out of his pocket, ripped it open and quickly slid a condom over his erection. He ripped off her thong, spread her legs and drove into her.

Parker gripped his shoulders, moaning. He gripped her ass and pulled her forward, holding her in place as he slid in and out of her wetness.

"I've missed my pussy, baby. I see it's been waiting for

me and my cock, isn't that right?" He ground into her. "Isn't that right?" he demanded.

"Yes, Mickey, I've missed your cock."

"You know no one can fill you like I can, no one can make you happy like this cock."

"Yes, no one. Just you, Mickey."

"Good girl, Parker. Who does this pussy belong to? Who do these tits belong to?"

"You, Mickey, only you."

"That's right, baby, mine. They are mine."

He leaned forward and took one of her nipples in his mouth, sucking and nipping it. He released her ass, and brought her knees up to her chest. He pushed into her deeper than before, stretching her even wider. He released one knee and started to rub her clit.

"You're going to come for me, baby. You're going to come on my cock. Your pussy is going to squeeze every last drop out of my cock. Are you listening to me?"

"Yes, Mickey," she panted. She could feel her body tensing, her orgasm building.

"Come on, baby, come for me," he demanded.

Parker fell apart. She moaned as her pussy clenched around his cock. Her clit was throbbing from his fingers. Her nipples were rock hard. She tried to close her legs but Mickey was there between them, holding them wider apart as he drove relentlessly into her. He was chasing his orgasm now. He gripped her breast and drove into her; he had no control. His forehead was on hers, his mouth an inch from hers, grunting with every push.

"Fuck me hard, Mickey," Parker moaned. Her tongue

licked his lips. "Claim that pussy, show me who's pussy it is."

"It's mine, baby. Mine." His grip on her breast tightened. His thrusts became labored. One push, then another and he roared as he came, spasming into her.

He collapsed against her. She wrapped her arms around him, waiting for his breathing to return to normal.

Mickey stood and pulled Parker off the counter, sliding her naked body down his before setting her on her feet and kissing her tenderly on the mouth. Parker took his hand and led him down a hall to the bathroom and into the shower.

Under the warm water Mickey picked up the soap and washed them both. He turned off the water, walked her out the shower, and dried them both.

It had been a long day and a long night. Parker was exhausted. She led the way into her bedroom and climbed onto the bed. Mickey lay down and pulled her to his side. She lay on him, snuggled into his side. He took her hand, put it on his chest, and then put his hand on top of hers. They were asleep in minutes.

CHAPTER 22
Mickey

He woke slowly to the sound of birds singing. He felt rested. More rested than he had in a long time. He knew why. The reason was still snuggled into his side. He lay still savoring the feel of her body pressed up against him, the even sound of her breathing, the smoothness of her skin under his hand.

He slid out from under her and quietly left the bedroom, going to the kitchen to find his clothes and put them on. He saw the coffee maker, found the coffee and started a pot. He picked up his phone while the coffee ran through the machine. He texted Toby, arranging to meet him for lunch.

He needed to go back to his hotel to get his laptop, although he had arranged to be away from the office, there was still work to be done. He didn't want to leave here without seeing Parker and making some plans with her.

When the coffee was done, he poured a cup and sat on the back patio scrolling through his phone, enjoying the peaceful quiet of her backyard.

Parker joined him about an hour later, wearing a large

T-shirt. She sat on his lap, putting her arms around his neck, bringing her lips to his.

"I thought you left," she said.

"Nope. I didn't want to leave without making plans." He nuzzled her neck. "Are you free tonight? I want to see you again."

"Aren't you going home?"

"Not tonight. I'm going to be spending more time here. I'm meeting Toby for lunch, see if he'll put me up for a while until I get my own place."

"You're going to move here?"

"I'm going to be where my girl is, baby." He caught her chin, pulling her face to his, watching her reaction to his words.

"But your business is on the east coast, your house..."

He cut her off, "But not my girl. Parker, did you not hear me last night? I want us to be together. I don't need to be where my business is. I have good people working for me. I will have to go there, but I don't need to live there. We'll figure it out."

"If you want us to be together, why are you going to ask Toby if you can stay with him. You know I have guest room." She smiled coyly at him.

"I'm not staying in your guest room, baby." He smiled at the disappointment on her face. "I'm staying in your room. With you."

Parker squealed. She threw her arms around his neck, kissing him. She sat back and said, "Closet space is going to be a problem, you know that."

"How much closet space do you need for all those bikinis, baby?" He was confused.

She slapped his chest. "That's not all I wear. I wear other clothes too."

"Too bad." He smirked.

She stood and then sat so she straddled him. She leaned forward and kissed him, teasing his lips with her tongue. He opened his mouth, letting her in. He fisted her hair, moving her head to allow him better access to her mouth.

She took his free hand and put it on her ass. She wasn't wearing any underwear. He groaned as he slid his hand around her body to her mound. He circled her clit then slid his finger down her folds. She was wet for him. She stood, undid his pants and pulled his cock out. She held him in her hand and sank onto him.

He stopped her. "Condom, baby," he ground out.

"I'm on the pill, Rod," she said as she dropped down taking all of him in. He slid his hands under her T-shirt, finding her breasts. They sat motionless, his cock filling her pussy, his hands on her tits. "Kiss me," she commanded.

He brought his lips to hers. She began to slowly rock on his lap. He dropped his hands to her ass, holding her there as she rocked. He leaned his head back watching as she fucked herself on his cock. Her eyes were closed, her hands on the back of the chair. "That's a good girl, baby. Use that cock. Take what you want because it's yours." He leaned forward and pulled a nipple into his mouth, wetting her T-shirt.

She hummed. He moved his mouth to her other nipple.

The cool air on her wet T-shirt made her nipple tighten even more.

"Mickey," she whined. She dropped her head onto his shoulder.

"What, baby? What do you want? Tell me," he ordered.

"Rub my clit, Mickey, please. Help me," she begged him.

He moved his hand to the front of her body again, finding her clit. With a firm hand he circled her clit as he started to push into her. "Is this what you want, baby?" he asked.

She couldn't answer, her orgasm was building, the walls of her pussy tightening around his cock. He pushed into her as she rocked on his lap. Her pussy was so wet and smooth. He was going to come. He held back the pleasure building in his body. He waited for her but he didn't have to wait long.

"Oh my God," she whispered into his neck as she climaxed. He held her and shot his seed into her as her pussy clenched his cock.

$$$

"Bro," Toby greeted him when he was ushered to Mickey's table.

Mickey stood and embraced Toby. "Good to see you again, Toby," he said.

They sat, ordered drinks and picked up their menus. "You weren't happy to see me last night," Toby said.

"Yeah, I was closing a deal, I didn't have time to talk to you."

"You were closing a deal with Parker Chen? What kind of a deal, bro? Why didn't you tell me you were coming to town?"

"I came to see Parker. If things didn't turn out the way I wanted them to I would have left without seeing you."

Two beers and mugs were put on the table in front of them. They placed their orders, poured some beer into their mugs, and clinked their glasses together before taking a drink.

"I'm missing something, Mickey. What kind of a deal are you doing with Parker?"

"The kind of deal where I'm moving in with her and spending more time in L.A." He couldn't keep the smile off his face as he looked at Toby.

"No! You and Parker! I knew there was something between you two. Fuck me, the mighty Mickey Finn is in love."

"That's a big word, Toby, I'm not sure we should be tossing it around at this early stage."

"You don't love her?"

He took a long drink. "I like her a lot. More than a lot. I think she could possibly be the one for me. It's early days, Toby. She has some stuff she has to work out and I have to give her time and space to come to her senses and realize I'm the only man she will ever need."

"Wow, Mickey, I'm happy for you. She'll be yours. How could she not fall for the Finn charm? You know I have that too. It's a blessing and a curse, man," Toby smirked.

"Rock star! Is the weight of all those women, holding you down?" Mickey snorted.

"You have no idea, bro," Toby finished his beer and motioned for two more.

$$\$\$\$$

Mickey knocked on Parker's door, suitcase and computer bag in hand. Parker opened the door wearing a sundress that fell to several inches above her knee.

"Yes?" she asked with a huge smile on her face.

"Is there a Parker Chen here?"

"Yes, you are speaking to her."

"You ordered a good-looking charming man to fill your every need?"

"Yes. Yes, I did," she said as she peered around him. "Is he here? Did you bring him with you?"

"I did, Ms. Chen. If you'll let me in, I can go over the operating instructions with you before I bring him in."

She stepped aside holding the door open. "Please come in," she said.

Mickey stepped into the foyer. Parker closed the door and turned to him. He took her in his arms and kissed her. "I missed you," he said.

Parker returned his embrace, snuggling against him. "I'll make supper. Why don't I give you a tour and then you can unpack."

They started in the master suite where Mickey dropped

his suitcase and bag. They stopped at the next door on the way back to the kitchen. Parker opened the door. "This is one of the guest rooms, an option for your office," she said as Mickey leaned into the room for a brief look around.

"Next door is an identical guest room, then the guest bathroom, and we are in the kitchen. If you look to the left, that is where you fucked me silly last night." She turned and hugged him, lifting her face to his for a kiss. He brushed his lips against hers.

She released him and turned to continue the tour. The other half of the house held the living room with a small sunroom and small extra room. "This is really too small for a bedroom so I use it as a library but this is another option for your office, Mickey."

She led him back to the kitchen and out onto the patio. "Patio," she said "and that," she pointed to the back of the yard to a building that could have been a garage or a large shed, "is where I practice. Come on, let me show you." Parker took his hand and they walked through the yard.

As they got closer to the building Mickey noticed that it was a newer build, newer than the house, and that it had quite a few security features on it. The windows had alarms, there were cameras covering all angles of the building and motion activated lights on every corner of the building. She had a fob on a wristband. She held it up to a box by the door. A beep signaled that the lock on the door had opened.

She opened the door and as she entered lights turned on. The room was cool, the walls were covered with sound proofing. In the center of the room, taking up the majority of space, was her kit. He imagined that there was a basic kit at the centre of the set up but arranged in a semicircle were more drums and cymbals. He was pretty sure that once she sat behind her kit, he would not be able to see her.

There was a couch, a fridge, and a small bar with a sink and a coffee machine.

"I don't bring a lot of people in here," she said as she pulled him down onto the couch. "I like it in here. It's quiet if I'm not drumming, a great place to relax and think."

"I like it, baby," he said as he leaned back on the couch, putting his arm around her shoulders.

"Did you have lunch with Toby?" she asked.

"Yes."

"How is he? Were the other guys there too?"

"No, just us. He's fine, a little pissed I didn't tell him I was coming."

"Why didn't you tell him you were coming?"

"Because I came to see you. I was just going to leave without telling him if things didn't work out between us."

"Really?"

"Really. If you had turned me down, baby I would not have been in the mood to visit."

"Good thing I agreed then."

"Good thing, but, really, you didn't stand a chance, baby. I had many more levels of charming I was going to unleash on your delicious little ass." He smirked at her.

"You don't say."

"Oh, I say, Parker Chen. You were a goner and you didn't even realize it." He laughed.

CHAPTER 23
Parker

The next few weeks seemed to fly by. Although Parker had never seen her life as lacking, she could not believe how happy she was all the time now. She and Mickey worked their way through sharing her house and a life without much adjustment. She learned a lot about herself that actually surprised her.

For instance, she liked cooking for her man. That domestic goddess shit that she had always scoffed at, well, she wasn't scoffing anymore. She liked taking care of Mickey and doing little things for him. She found out that she liked sex in the morning. There was nothing like starting the day off with a good orgasm from one of the sexiest men she had ever met.

What surprised her the most was how happy she was with the consistency of Mickey. Always waking up with him, either in her bed or in the house. He was always there with her and if he wasn't she knew where he was. She never had to agonize over whether he liked her or appreciated her. She was constantly being showered with his affection, hugs, kisses, little pats on her ass.

As the days and weeks went by the one thing that she had worried about more than anything was put to rest. She was happy with just one cock, Mickey's cock. She didn't miss the variety she used to have, the revolving door of men and meaningless encounters. Mickey fulfilled her in ways she didn't think anyone ever could.

$$$

Mickey was making coffee. They had just come out of the bedroom. Parker sat at the island fully appreciating his ass in his black knit boxers. Mickey pushed the brew button and turned to catch Parker looking at his ass, now his cock.

"Like what you see, baby?" he asked with a smirk on his face.

"Oh yeah, Rod," she said as she met his gaze. "You make me hot for your rod, Hot Rod."

He laughed at her. Suddenly his gaze flew over her shoulder and his face hardened into a menacing glower.

"What?" she squealed as she spun around. Colin Columbo stood in the doorway to the kitchen.

"Well, this is awkward," he said.

"Colin!" Parker exclaimed at the same time that Mickey barked out, "How the hell did you get in the house?"

Parker jumped off her chair and walked toward Colin, putting herself between Mickey and Colin.

"I have a key," he said to Mickey, jutting his chin out to emphasize that he was entitled to be here.

"What the fuck?" Mickey said.

"He has a key, Mickey," Parker blurted out, trying to

calm him down, sensing his anger. "I gave him a key." She turned to Colin "What are you doing here?"

"You weren't answering me, Parker. I've been texting and calling for a couple of weeks and…"

"Maybe she doesn't want to answer you," Mickey said. "That ever occur to you?"

"Please, Mickey," Parker said, looking over her shoulder, "I'll take care of this." She turned back to Colin. "I've been busy, Colin. Is everything okay?"

"Yeah, yeah," he said. Looking over her shoulder at Mickey, he put a hand on her arm. "I'm just missing you, boo," he whispered.

"If you don't get your hands off her…" Mickey yelled.

"Mickey, please," Parker said to him again. She moved her arm out of Colin's hold and pushed him backward, back toward the front door of the house. "You have to go, Colin."

Colin resisted Parker's push. "Who is that guy?"

Parker pushed him again. "Colin, please," she said. She put her hand on his shoulder, turning him away from the kitchen and Mickey, toward the front of the house.

"Who is he, Parker?" Colin asked again as he walked toward the front door.

"He's Mickey Finn, Colin. I'm with him now. You can't just come over anymore," she said as she leaned past him and opened the front door.

"C'mon, Parker, we have something special, don't we? I wanted to spend some time with you. I'm missing my boo." He leaned forward to kiss her, nuzzle her neck.

Parker put her hand on his chest, keeping him away

from her. "I'm with Mickey, Colin. *I'm with him.*" She stressed the words, hoping to get through to him.

"But…"

"There is no but, Colin. Mickey lives with me. We're together. You can't just come over anymore." She held out her hand, palm upward. "The key, Colin. I need it back."

Colin pouted and took a moment to take the key off his keyring and give it to her. "What if you guys don't work out? I'll need that key back. You'll want me to have it back."

Parker smiled at him. "if that ever happens, which is not likely, I'll give you another key."

She gently pushed him out the door and closed it behind him. She leaned against it for a moment, dreading having to face Mickey and deal with the questions that were coming.

Mickey was bracing himself against the island. He glared at her as she entered the kitchen. She walked past him and poured two cups of coffee, one for her and one for Mickey. She placed his cup on the island and went to the fridge to put cream in her cup.

She came back to Mickey's side, put her cup on the island beside his and ducked under his arm, pushing him away from the island. He stood and she wrapped her arms around him, resting her cheek on his chest. She didn't say anything.

He was stiff and unyielding under her touch. She stood her ground. He brought one arm up, and then the other, wrapping his arms around her. He bent down and kissed her head.

"How many other keys are out there, baby?" he asked, resignation in his voice.

"Two more, Mickey," she answered honestly.

"We're changing the locks today." There was no leeway for argument in his voice.

"Yes, Mickey. That's a good idea," she agreed.

He slid his hands down her back, grabbed her ass, and lifted her onto the island. He stood between her spread legs, looking into her eyes. "I don't share," he said.

"I know, Mickey." She leaned forward and brushed her lips against his chin. She raised her hand and slid it through his hair, pulling his head down to her. "I know," she said as she brushed her lips over his. "I know." She wrapped her legs around his waist, pulling him into her.

She heard him exhale the breath he had been holding. She felt the tension leave his body. She snuggled into his body. He wrapped his arms around her, holding her tightly to him. They stayed like that, not speaking, letting the matter settle and dissipate. He exhaled another large breath, giving her a quick squeeze, before stepping away from her and pulling her off the island.

"Plans for today?" he asked.

She picked up her mug. "Coffee first, then practice." She took a sip. "I'm going to call Brynn and see what she is up to, maybe meet her for lunch. Want to join?"

"I'd love to, but I've got some calls to make and some emails to go through." He hooked his arm around her, pulling her up against his side. "What about later? Want to go out for drinks? I can ask Toby if he wants to get together."

"Sounds great, Mickey. Call Toby about tonight."

"Okay," he slid his hand down her back and patted her ass. He looked down at her, smiling "I lo—" he seemed to catch himself, not finishing his thought.

She met his eyes and raised her eyebrows.

"I'll look for a locksmith, get those locks changed today," he said.

Two hours later Mickey was waiting for the locksmith as she left to meet Brynn for lunch.

$$$

Parker slid into the booth opposite Brynn at their favorite diner. "Where's Saint?" she asked, surprised that he wasn't there.

"He's finally had enough of L.A. He flew back home. I really don't expect to see him for a couple months."

"What is it with you two anyway, Brynn? Are you with him? You always seem to be annoyed when he is around, but he is always around. Tell me, this inquiring mind needs to know," Parker begged.

"I don't even know what we are, Parker. He is always with me yes, but we are not together. I've never slept with him and he doesn't even seem to be interested in sex with me. I am annoyed when he is around because he is in my life and I can't figure out why and that bugs me." She sighed an exasperated sigh. "But enough about me, what is going on with you and Mickey?"

"Well," Parker began as she leaned across the table with a smile on her face.

"What'd'll ya have girls," Juanita, the waitress, asked as she came to the table with a pad and pen in her hands.

"We'll have the usual, Juanita," Brynn replied. "You don't even have to ask."

"I know," she replied with a smile. "I was just testing you two. How ya been?"

"Good," Parker and Brynn answered at the same time.

"Just busy," Brynn continued.

"You and everybody else," Juanita responded. "Where is that tall drink of cocoa you are usually carrying around with you?" Juanita looked at Brynn.

"He's gone back home for a couple of months. Do you miss him, Juanita? Should I send him your kisses when he calls?" Brynn teased.

"Don't go doing me any favors, girl," Juanita huffed, "but if he asks…oh, never mind." She turned and walked to the kitchen to place their order. Brynn and Parker watched her walk away with stunned looks on their faces.

"Juanita and Saint?" Parker said.

"Crazier things have happened," Brynn said.

"Yes, they have," Parker agreed.

Juanita was back at their table with their order. "Two sundaes, two Cokes, and two coffees," she said as she placed the items on the table.

"Thank you," Parker and Brynn said.

They each picked up their spoons, dug into their sundaes and slid the ice cream into their mouths. They wore identical looks of bliss on their faces as they closed their eyes, savoring the taste.

"Okay," Brynn spoke first, "tell me all about you and Mickey."

Parker took another spoonful of ice cream and then said, "Brynn, I have been so happy. I don't get it. I love to cook for the man and take care of him, like some throwback to the fifties. I am personally sending feminism back seventy years and I am not ashamed."

"I'm so happy for you, Parker. I was pulling for you and Mickey. He seems like such a nice guy."

"He is. He's super nice and he treats me good." Another spoonful of ice cream. "He is so sexy, too. I orgasm at least three or four times a day."

"First of all," Brynn said sternly, "too much information. Second, now you're just bragging, bitch!"

"I know, right? I feel like my life is a musical and I should be dancing and singing all the time."

"You're in the honeymoon phase, Parker. It's how you deal with mundane day-to-day life that's the true test. It's not always song and dance. Enjoy it while you can."

"Colin came over this morning," Parker said, her voice lowering to a whisper.

"What? What do you mean he came over?"

"I've been friends with benefits with him for so long I gave him a key. Mickey and I were in the kitchen this morning when Colin just walked in. Thank goodness we both had our clothes on. If you only knew what goes on in that kitchen."

"Eww, I don't think I'll ever come over for supper again." Brynn smirked. "What happened when Colin popped up?"

"Mickey was upset."

"Really? Go figure."

"Colin was being a jerk and sort of riling Mickey up. There were a few tense moments but I got Colin to leave. Right now, Mickey is waiting for a locksmith to come and change the locks."

"So, what happened after Colin left?"

"Nothing. Mickey was upset, of course, but he just let it go. It's not like I didn't have a life before I met him."

"Wow," Brynn said, "and he didn't mention anything about your past? Didn't throw it in your face?"

"How could he? It's not like he was a celibate angel before I met him."

"I admire that about him, Parker."

"Brynn, I am developing feelings for him."

"Feelings?"

"Yeah, like serious feelings."

"Serious feelings?"

"I think I might be on the verge of love."

At that moment Parker's cell chimed. She picked up her phone and looked at the text. "The locks are changed," she said to Brynn. "We're meeting his brother for drinks later. Why don't you join us? You know Toby."

"Well…"

"Oh, come on! You don't have anything to do with your spare time now that Saint has gone back home."

"I want you to know that that is not true. I do have a life outside of Saint, but, yes, I will join you. Where are we going?"

"I don't know." Parker texted Mickey back. A moment later she said, "The Moonlight Oasis."

"Well, then drink up, girlfriend," Brynn said, "we have some shopping to do."

CHAPTER 24
Mickey

"Holy shit," Toby exclaimed. "All you did was change the locks?"

"What did you expect me to do?" Mickey asked with annoyance.

"I don't know, bro, kick his ass out of the house."

"Parker had a life before me. The problem was hers to handle and she did it well. I would have stepped in if it had developed into a problem."

"You're right," Toby agreed, "that was the smart thing to do. There's a reason you're the big brother."

Toby and Mickey were standing at a table in the Moonlight Oasis waiting for Parker. Despite its fanciful name, the Oasis was a neighborhood bar that had aged well. Toby and the band were regulars here and weren't bothered often by the odd fan that happened to come in. The bartenders also looked after them, ensuring that they were treated like regular customers and not award-winning rockstars.

Mickey hadn't seen Parker since early in the afternoon and he was getting anxious. His life with her was so good.

There were moments when he couldn't believe that they were together. She never gave him any reason to doubt her, but their life before would occasionally rear its ugly head. Like now. Where was she? Was she going to stand him up? Would he see her later today or would she ghost him again?

He took another sip of his drink when he saw her enter the bar, and he wasn't the only one. Mickey felt as if every man in the place zeroed in on his girl the moment she walked through the door. And why not? She was stunning.

She was wearing some floaty, gauzy floral dress that seemed to whisper around her, highlighting her bronze complexion, her almond eyes, and her black hair. Brynn was right behind her, but Mickey's eyes returned to Parker. She scanned the bar and when she saw him her face lit up. She was happy to see him.

She was at his side in a moment, putting her arms around him, pulling him down for a kiss and a whisper: "You are extra sexy tonight, Mr. Finn. I can hardly wait to get home to suck your big cock."

He slid his hand down her back, patting her on the ass. "You too, Ms. Chen. I like your dress but I would prefer to see it on the bedroom floor."

She laughed a husky laugh. "Wait until you see what's under this dress. Brynn and I went shopping." She arched an eyebrow at him.

"Maybe we should just leave now." He smiled at her.

She smacked him in the chest. "We just got here!"

"Okay, in half an hour then."

"No."

He picked up her hand and kissed her knuckles. She

turned to Brynn and Toby. "Toby, what have you been up to? Where are the rest of the guys?" Mickey was doing something to her wrist while he held her hand.

"LeShawn and Marcus are coming. Silvio is on a date, but he said he still might join us later if things don't go the way he wants them to." He smirked.

Parker laughed. "Brynn, what do you think that means?"

"I think we all know what that means, Parker." Brynn laughed. "Let's go get some drinks."

"Good idea," Parker agreed as she lifted her hand to brush her hair back. There was a silver chain on her wrist, a pendant dangling from it. She looked at it with confusion on her face. She took the pendant in her other hand. It was a diamond-encrusted heart. It was beautiful. She looked at Mickey. He was smiling.

"Do you like it, baby?"

"Mickey, it's beautiful, but I can't accept this."

"Yes, you can," he said.

"But it's so expensive, I don't deserve this."

He pulled her into his arms. "You do deserve it. I want you to have it, I lo—" He caught himself before continuing his thought.

"You what?" Parker asked.

"I thought of you when I saw it. It looks good on you." He kissed her. "I want you to have it."

"Okay," she said, "but this is the last one, Mickey. I mean it."

"I make no promises."

"Okay, you two," Brynn broke into their conversation, "I'm thirsty. Come on, Parker, let's go get a drink."

Mickey and Toby watched them walk toward the bar.

"That was a nice piece of jewelry, bro," Toby observed.

Brynn had Parker's wrist in her hand, looking at the bracelet while they waited for their drinks.

"I almost bought her a ring," Mickey said.

"No," Toby said.

"Yes, Toby. I love her." Mickey felt a weight lift off his shoulders after admitting his feelings to another person.

"No shit? Have you told her?"

"No, I want to, but I don't know how she would react. I don't want to scare her. I don't know if she's ready to hear it."

"Do you think she feels the same way,"

"How can she not?" he joked. "I don't know. I don't even know what signs to look for, Toby. I haven't been here before."

"You're right though, Mickey. How can she not love you, too? I think she does. Maybe she doesn't know it yet or maybe she doesn't want to acknowledge it but the way she looks at you—it's written all over her face."

Brynn and Parker came to the table carrying their drinks. Parker had an extra drink that she placed in front of Mickey. "I got you a refill," she said.

"You know, baby, you are going to get lucky tonight. You don't have to get me drunk." He smiled at her. "Just sayin'."

"I just want to know you're a sure thing for later, Rod." She winked at him.

"T.M.I., you two," Brynn said. "Let's talk about something else besides you two fucking."

"Hear, hear," Toby chimed in as he clinked his glass with Brynn's.

CHAPTER 25
Parker

She was in the ladies' room, fixing her make up, waiting for Brynn. The bracelet caught her attention again. It was so beautiful and such a surprise.

She heard her mother's voice. "Is that silver? Not gold. Maybe it's platinum, that would be the best. You should tell him you want platinum. The pendant is nice. I wonder if they make them bigger with more diamonds. Ask him if you can get a bigger one. If he loves you, he would do it."

She shook her head, trying to push her mother out of her head. Mickey doesn't love her. Sure, he likes her, likes her a lot, but love, no. That was why she didn't want to accept such an extravagant piece of jewelry from him. She didn't want him to regret the gift when they broke up. She didn't want to have to fight about it and end up throwing it at him when they were over. But she loved it and she wanted it. She would enjoy it while she could.

Brynn joined her at the mirror, looking at her make up, opening her bag and refreshing her lip gloss. "The diamonds on that thing are hypnotizing," she said to Parker.

"Yeah," she agreed. "I know what my mother would say though."

"Don't do that, Parker. Don't spoil this gift from a man who has feelings for you."

"I know, it's just hard not to hear her at times like this."

"Just remember that you don't want to be like her." Brynn threw her lip gloss back in her bag and snapped it shut. "C'mon, your man is waiting for you. Let's have some fun." She hooked her arm through Parker's and pulled her toward the door.

They returned to the table. LeShawn had joined the table and Marcus was just walking into the bar. A band was walking onto the small stage in the corner. Parker slipped under Mickey's arm. He pulled her against his side, leaving his hand on her hip.

"Money, I was surprised when Toby said you were moving here," LeShawn said. "I hope we are going to hang out more often now."

"Yeah," Marcus agreed. "What made you want to make the move? Isn't your business on the east coast?"

Mickey took a sip of his drink before replying. "I'm moving here to be with my girl." He looked down at Parker who returned his gaze.

Marcus and LeShawn exchanged a look and then they both looked at Toby who nodded his head.

"You and Parker? No shit," Marcus said.

Mickey just smiled as Parker wrapped her arms around his waist.

"Yeah, I can see it, man," LeShawn said. "So, what's

next? Marriage? Babies? Or is it going to be babies and then marriage?"

Parker laughed. "Let's put the brakes on that real fast, LeShawn! You first."

LeShawn held his hands up in front of himself, palms outward, "Let's not go talking crazy talk, Parker. There's way too much pussy out there that I haven't met yet."

The band started playing. The music was loud and the tunes were catchy. Parker turned to watch them play. They guys talked and laughed as the beer flowed freely.

The band took a break and came to their table. Toby and the other Temptation members knew them.

"Hey, Gar," Toby called to the drummer, "this is Parker Chen." He said as he pointed to Parker. "Parker, this is Gar."

Parker smiled at Gar. Gar moved to stand beside her. "Wow! Great to meet you, Parker. I read your interview in *Beats* magazine."

"Okay," she replied.

Gar moved closer. He put his hard on her lower back. He picked up his beer, took a drink, then leaned in to say something to her.

A hand snaked around her waist and pulled her backward and to the side. Suddenly Mickey was standing in front of Gar, glaring at him. "No need to touch her," he said.

Gar took a step back, holding out his hands, palms outward. "No problem, man. I didn't know she was with you."

"She is with me. Keep your hands to yourself."

Parker watched the exchange. "Mickey, can I speak to you please?" she asked.

"No need, baby, just having a word with your new friend here," he replied, not taking his eyes off Gar.

"Mickey," she took his hand in hers, "now, please." She put her other hand on his arm and pulled him.

"What?" he snapped.

"Come here," she snapped back at him as she pulled him toward the back of the bar, down a darkly-lit hall leading to the bathrooms. She walked past the doors to the end of the hall. She turned, pulling Mickey with her and slammed him against the wall.

"Parker—" he began.

She pushed her body up against his. "Are you taking care of me, Rod?" She slid her fingers through his hair and pulled his face down to hers, claiming his lips in a passionate kiss. "Making sure no one else gets this pussy?"

"That pussy is mine, baby, and you know it." He growled at her.

He was so sexy. He was such a man and he took care of her. It was such a turn on when he told Gar to keep his hands to himself.

Mickey stood still; he had not been expecting this. She knew he had expected a lecture on being nice to people.

With her knee, Parker spread his legs apart and began to rub herself against him. Mickey lifted his leg, putting his foot against the wall. He claimed her lips and took control of the kiss, pushing his tongue into her mouth. He put his hands on her waist and held her as she rubbed against him.

She grabbed his shirt. "You are so fucking sexy. You

make me so wet. I can't control myself," she whispered as she sped her gyrations on his leg.

"Take what you want, baby," he whispered, exhaling into her ear before licking her delicately there.

Parker shivered and moaned in response. She lifted the front of her dress out from between her legs. She pushed her thong to the side. Her clit was directly on the rough denim of Mickey's jeans. She gripped his T-shirt tighter. "I'm going to come, Mickey."

Mickey held her, letting her ride his leg. Her eyes were half opened, her teeth biting into her lower lip. She started to hum. He knew she was going to explode; he grabbed her chin, forcing her face to his and kissed her, capturing her whimper as she came.

"Oh my God," she said as she collapsed against him.

Mickey put his foot down and pulled her up against him. Holding her while her breathing slowed and returned to normal. He took her hand in his and led her back to their table. He put his arm around her shoulders, pulling her into him for a kiss on her forehead.

Toby cleared his throat, drawing Mickey's attention. "Did you two just fuck in the bathroom hallway?"

Parker pushed her face into Mickey's chest. Mickey picked up his beer, took a sip, looked at Toby, and said, "Something like that."

Toby laughed. "You lucky dog."

"You have no idea, bro. None." He slid his arm down Parker's back, grabbed her ass, and gave it a little pat.

$$$

It was a week later when Parker came home from the studio. Mickey was on the back patio with a water, scrolling through his phone, where she joined him.

"Baby, I've got to go home for a bit," he said, as he put his phone down and met her eyes.

"Aw, do you have to?"

"I do, but just for a little while."

"How long, Mickey?"

"No more than a week. Come with me."

"I can't. I'm scheduled to be in the studio for this week and next. When are you leaving?"

"My flight is tomorrow morning at ten. Come here, baby."

Parker stood and took the two steps to him. He took her hand in his and pulled her onto his lap. She leaned against him.

"Let's go out for dinner," he said. "I'll buy you cake for your dessert."

"For my dessert? What about yours?"

"You're always my dessert, baby."

She laughed. "Do you deserve dessert tonight, Rod?"

"I deserve dessert every night," he replied with a smile.

"You do, Rod, you do."

$$$

Dinner had been nice, nothing fancy. The cake, however, was exquisite. They were back at home, the sweat drying from their bodies after Mickey's dessert. She was straddling him on the couch, leaning against his chest.

Mickey, had her breast in his hand, absentmindedly massaging it. "Another night where we didn't make it to the bedroom," he said as he kissed her forehead.

"You were in a hurry to have your dessert." She giggled.

"Always in a hurry for you, baby. I can't help myself." He pinched her nipple.

"Uhmm," Parker responded, arching her back and pushing her breast into his hand.

"Everything about you is perfect, perfect for me," he said as he nuzzled her neck.

"Do you know what I think, Mickey?"

"Tell me, baby."

"I think you should have seconds for dessert." She trailed her hand down, stroking his cock. She slid off the couch, kneeling between his legs. She took his cock in her hands and brought it to her mouth. She kissed the tip. "Let me take care of this for you, Rod," she said with a smile.

Mickey fisted her hair. "You know it's yours, baby. You can have some if you want."

"Oh, I want, Rod." She licked the underside of his cock up from his balls to the tip. She poked her tongue into the hole, then swirled her tongue around the head.

Mickey lifted his hips and pulsed upward.

Parker opened her mouth, sliding him all the way in to the back of her throat. She held him there for a moment before slowly pulling upward. Her free hand found his balls and began to massage them.

Mickey moaned and leaned back against the couch; his eyes closed. He pushed her head down on his cock. She slid her mouth down his length. With a gentle tug on her hair, he urged her head up. Parker took over. She popped him out of her mouth and took him in her hand. Mickey put his hand over hers, guiding her as he began to stroke himself. She licked the head of his cock and Mickey picked up the pace, stroking himself faster and harder.

He sat up, leaning forward, forcing Parker back on her heels. He pumped his cock and shot his cum onto her face and then down to her tits. Parker stuck her tongue out, lapping up the cum on her face. Mickey released his cock, leaned forward and rubbed it into her chest, over her tits.

"You are going to kill me, baby," he said as he claimed her lips. "I'm a dead man."

She laughed and took his hand. "C'mon, let's take a bath, Rod."

"It has to be a shower, Parker. I want to pack a few things tonight before bed."

$$$

They lay in bed the next morning, cuddling post-orgasm. Parker rolled away from him, stretching, reaching her hands over her head.

"I've got to leave in forty-five minutes, Mickey. Do you want breakfast?"

"Sure, how about a couple eggs and some toast. I'm going to get dressed and finish packing."

Parker slid out of bed, picked up his T-shirt from last night, and slipped it over her head. This was her usual morning attire. She padded out of the bedroom toward the kitchen.

$$$

Breakfast was over, Parker was dressed and they were getting ready to leave; Mickey to the airport and Parker to the studio. They stood in the foyer, wrapped in each other's arms.

"I want you to think about something while I'm away, baby," Mickey said.

"Okay," Parker said, smiling up at him.

"I love you," he said, watching her face.

Parker giggled at him, then realized that he was serious. Her body tensed against his. She stepped out of his arms.

"I wasn't expecting that, Rod," she confessed.

"I just want you to think about it, baby, and know that that's how I feel about you. There is nothing to be scared of. Nothing is going to change between us." He was speaking quickly, trying to say as many things as he could think of that would keep her calm. Trying to keep her with him and not send her running out the door.

"Okay." She pasted a smile on her face. "I'll think about it while you're gone." She was freaking the fuck out on the inside.

"I'll call you tonight, Parker. We can talk about this. Or not. I'll speak to you later, okay?" he asked.

"Okay," she said through her teeth. She just wanted him to leave.

Outside, a car honked. "That's my Uber. I've got to go," he said as he took her into his arms one last time and kissed her. "I love you, Parker," he said again before he opened the door and left.

Parker fell forward, her hands on her knees. Why was it so hot in here all of a sudden? She couldn't seem to get enough air into her lungs. He loved her. Mickey loved her.

She heard her mother's voice in her head: "Good work, Parker. He loves you. You have what you need now."

"No," she said. She stood and put her hands on her back, walking back into the house. "No, I'm not like that," she said aloud. She walked a few laps around the living room, trying to slow her breathing, trying to get her mother's voice out of her head. She sat on the couch with her head in her hands.

Her phone rang. She pulled it out of her purse. Fuck, was that the time? She was late. She took the call from the producer she was working with. "Yeah, Seth, I had some car trouble this morning. I'm almost there. I didn't think I would be late. I'm sorry, really, really sorry. I'm almost there." She ended the call and ran out the door.

CHAPTER 26
Mickey

Mickey was not surprised by Parker's reaction. Of course, he had hoped that she would be happy and maybe tell him that she loved him, too, but nope. Didn't happen. When he got to the airport, he almost turned around to go back home and wait for Parker, but his presence was required on the east coast and he would just have to go home as soon as possible after dealing with those urgent matters.

On the plane he read reports, dealt with emails, anything to keep his mind off Parker. Once he touched down Tony picked him up at the airport and took him straight to the office and into one of many meetings scheduled for the day. By the time his meetings were over Tony brought him to his hotel after going through a drive thru, it was nine.

Mickey took off his jacket, loosened his tie and dialed Parker's cell. He opened his take-out bag in the glistening kitchen of the penthouse he had rented as the phone rang. He popped the top off his keto bowl and took a fork out of the utensil drawer when his call went to voicemail. He disconnected and immediately dialed again. He left a message this time.

"Don't do this, baby. Talk to me, damn it. Tell me what is going on in that beautiful head of yours." He ended the call and texted her immediately.

Mickey: *Call me baby. Please don't do this again.*

Parker didn't call him that night. When he woke the next morning after a fitful sleep he checked his phone, still nothing. He tried to stay calm, tried to imagine all the reasons why she didn't call him last night, or return his text. The only good reason he came up with was Parker in a coma after being hit by a car. Yeah, let's not think that.

$$$

Parker

"I got here as soon as I could. What's the emergency?" Brynn asked as she slid into the booth across from Parker. She was alarmed when she looked at Parker. She had obviously not slept last night. Her eyes were red as if she had been crying. "Is it Mickey? Did something happen?"

"Oh my God," Parker said. She dropped her head to the table, bouncing it on the table top.

"What?" Brynn asked again as she pushed her hand under Parker's head, to keep it from banging on the table again. "You're scaring me. Fucking what!"

Parker abruptly sat up and then slumped back against the booth. "He loves me." Silent tears ran down her face.

"Who? Who loves you? Mickey?"

"Yes. He had to go back home. He told me just before he left. Brynn, what am I going to do?"

"You know, Parker, I seem to be missing something here. The man who has been living with you for the past several months, the man who treats you like a treasure, the man who seems to make you, like, really happy, told you he loved you? Is that what you are telling me?"

"Yes," Parker said

"You want to know what to do?"

"Yes."

"Can you possibly just accept his love? Maybe love him back? Is that too easy? Do you want something more complicated?"

"Don't use that tone on me, Brynn Williams," Parker warned.

"What tone? The tone that implies that maybe you're not as intelligent as you think you are? Because if that is the tone you are talking about, I think it is an appropriate tone for this occasion. I am the music producer at this table." Brynn smirked at Parker.

"Now you're making fun of me. You are laughing at my agony, Brynn. Some friend you are."

"What agony, sweetie? The man loves you. I say hu-fuckin-rah! You are one lucky bitch to have earned the love of a man like Mickey Finn, and you don't even appreciate it. Tell me why this is such a terrible thing."

"You know why."

"If I knew, I wouldn't be asking."

"Cuz, you know, what if he is the last man I ever have sex with? What if there is someone better than him for me?"

"Do you think there could be someone better for you out there?"

"I don't know. I don't think so. But you know I like variety."

"Do you? Didn't seem like you liked it that much before you met Mickey. When you came back to L.A. you didn't even look for any for six months. Be honest with yourself, Parker. What else? There has to be another reason."

"He told me he loved me and the next voice I heard was my mother's basically telling me I had him right where I wanted him. What if I am her?"

"You're not her. Don't let her spoil this wonderful thing for you."

"But what if I will turn into her? I had a front row seat to her method for years. How can I have not learned anything?"

Brynn reached across the table and took Parker's hands in hers. "You did learn a lot, you probably learned everything, but you have a mind of your own. You don't want to be like her so you won't be like her. You are not destined to walk in your mother's footsteps. As a matter of fact, Ms. Parker Chen, you are one of the most loyal, selfless, loving people I have ever met. Why do you think I'm your friend? Why do you think Mickey loves you?"

"I am pretty wonderful."

"You are."

"Yes I am."

"Let's keep the ego in check, Parker."

"Good evening, ladies," their waitress said. "Tonight's specials are meatloaf with mashed potatoes…."

"We know what we want," Brynn cut her off. Smiling at the waitress, she said, "Banana split, double toppings, two spoons."

Parker wiped her sleeve over her eyes and gave a watery smile to Brynn. "That's it, girlfriend, ain't nothin' a banana split, double toppings, can't solve."

$$$

Mickey

Another late night. He realized he had to come home to deal with these issues. Despite the fact that he would rather be in L.A. with Parker right now, he had to be here. It was almost eleven at night when he dialed Parker's cell. Her phone rang and rang, he was about to disconnect when she answered.

"Hello," her voice was heavy with sleep.

He smiled. "Did I wake you up, baby?"

"Mickey?"

"Yes, baby." He loved her like this, half asleep, half awake. If he was with her right now, he would be gently kissing her, rubbing her back.

"I miss you, Mickey. It's lonely here without you."

"I'll be home soon," he reassured her.

"Why not now?"

"Because I'm on the east coast, remember?"

"I remember that you love me." She was more awake now; he could tell from her voice.

"How do you feel about that?"

"Scared."

"Why scared, Parker?"

"That's a lot of responsibility you gave me, Mickey."

"How do you figure that?"

"You gave me the responsibility for your heart Mickey. That's a lot of power to give to someone, someone who may not deserve it, who shouldn't be trusted with it."

"I never thought of it like that. Lucky for me that I trust you with my heart."

"Maybe you shouldn't, Mickey. But I want you to know that I will take this responsibility seriously. I will protect your heart from me." She yawned.

"Are you working tomorrow?"

"I am." She yawned again.

"I'm going to let you go back to sleep, baby. I'll be home soon. I love you, Parker."

"Good night, Mickey," she said before she ended the call.

He didn't understand what she was talking about when she said she would protect his heart from herself. He'd have to try to unravel that mystery. Just not now. He was tired too. He had another full day tomorrow and he needed to get some sleep.

$$\$\$\$$$

Parker

It was quiet in the house. Mickey was not there and she really missed him. She missed his smile, his voice, just his presence. It occurred to her that she had never felt that way about any of the other men she had been with, not even

Colin. They had lived together for a short period of time and then on-again, off-again a number of times and she never missed him when he was gone. She was never anxious for Colin to finish a tour and come back to her, actually, there were even instances where she dreaded his coming back to her.

She picked up her cell and texted him.

Parker: *Hey.*

He responded immediately.

Mickey: *Morning baby. How are you?*

Parker: *Thinking of you.*

Mickey: *Naked?*

Parker: *(Snort) me or you?*

Mickey: *You tell me.*

Parker: *You of course.*

Mickey: *Am I fucking you?*

Parker: *No, but now that you mention it…*

Mickey: *Wish I was there.*

Parker: *Me too. I'm just going to have to get some battery-operated relief.*

Mickey: *I didn't need that image in my head right now, I'm just about to go into a meeting with the mayor.*

Parker: *Guess you better get there early so you can be sitting down when everyone else arrives.*

Mickey: *Good plan, baby. I love you.*

Parker: *Thank you.*

Mickey: *Thank you?*

Parker: *For now. I have to leave in 15 minutes, Mickey. I'll talk to you later.*

Mickey: *Okay.*

$$$

She arrived to an empty studio. A technician was waiting for her in the sound booth.

"Yeah, session's cancelled," he said.

"Just today?" Parker asked. She was booked for the next ten days to work on this project.

"Nope, the whole thing. Singer's husband served her with divorce papers or something."

"Oh. That's so sad," Parker said.

"Whatev," the technician said as he stood. "I'm done here now so I'm gonna lock up. Is there anything else you wanted?"

"No, I'm good," Parker said.

She sat in her car in the parking lot trying to decide what to do with her sudden free time. If Mickey were here, she would be hanging out with him. Brynn was working, so that was out. She didn't feel like shopping.

She felt as if she were suddenly on holidays. What did you do on holidays? Why, travel of course! She pulled her cell out of her purse and booked a flight. She had four hours to go home, pack, get to the airport and surprise Mickey when he got home tonight. She squealed. She was excited. She would see Mickey tonight!

She was going to tell him that she loved him, too, because, well, because she did, she realized it just now, as if struck by lightning. Not only did she love him now, she had loved him for a while, she just wouldn't allow herself to acknowledge it.

$$$

Parker stepped out of the Uber and pulled her case behind her to Mickey's front door. She knew the security code and was in the house in seconds. She closed the door hearing music blaring as she slipped off her shoes. That was odd, she thought Mickey was at work.

She left her case at the door and walked down the hallway into the living area. She walked to the kitchen counter and put down her purse.

"Who are you?" a woman's voice asked. "How did you get in? I'm going to call the police." The voice was escalating to hysteria with every word she spoke.

Parker spun around. There was a tall leggy blonde in the hallway to the bedroom. "Don't move," she said as she lifted her hand as if to stop Parker. She was wearing an over-large T-shirt, Mickey's T-shirt. When she lifted her arm the hem of the T-shirt raised to reveal a nude thong.

Parker's eyes looked over her shoulder. Was Mickey here? Was he in the bedroom. "Is Mickey here?" she asked.

"Yes, he is," she said, quickly looking over her shoulder.

"Can I speak to him?" Parker asked.

"He's busy. He's getting dressed. Who did you say you were?"

"Nobody," Parker responded. "I seem to have misunderstood something. I'm sorry if I scared you." She put her purse back on her shoulder. "I'll just go. I'll call Mickey later."

"Who should I tell him you are?"

"Nobody. Don't tell him I was here. I've made a terrible

mistake." Parker held it together long enough to spin around, put on her shoes, grab her case and run out of the house.

CHAPTER 27
Mickey

This was the second day that Parker was not answering his calls or his texts. His frustration with her was mounting. He told her he loved her and she seemed to be coming around. They had spoken three nights ago and texted the next morning. He thought things were moving in the right direction.

Meetings for the day were done. He was in his office doing paperwork, he wanted to speak to Parker, touch base, get his bearings, but she wasn't responding to him. His phone rang and he quickly picked it up. It was his cousin, Meeka.

"Hey, Meeks," he answered.

"Hi, Uncle Mickey," she greeted him with a super sweet voice.

"I know that tone, Meeks. What do you want?"

"Do you think I could use your card to go shopping?" she asked. She took a quick breath and barrelled ahead. "I'm going to go out on a date and he's taking me to a nice restaurant and I don't really have anything nice to wear…please?"

He laughed. "Yes, Meeks, don't max it out," he warned sternly. He had a black card, no limit, as if she could max it out but, somehow, he wouldn't put it past her. He loosened his tie and leaned back. "Are you enjoying the house?"

Meeka was his cousin but she called him Uncle because of their age difference. Meeka was young enough that she could have been his daughter. She had just graduated college and wanted to take some time off before starting her career and looking for work. She also wanted to get out of her parents' house and finally have some independence. She had initially asked if she could move in with him but that was just before he moved to L.A. so he let her have the house to herself. Since he was only going to be in town for a week or so he was staying in a hotel downtown close to his office.

"Great. I love it. I can't thank you enough for this, Uncle Mickey."

"It was nothing, Meeks. You are doing me a favor, living there while I am out of town. Everything working okay?"

"Yeah, no problems..." she paused, "except…"

"Except what?"

"Well, something weird happened a couple of days ago. I think one of your old girlfriends came to see you."

"What? Who?"

"She wouldn't give me her name, but she got into the house. She was in the kitchen when I woke up. She freaked me out."

"She was in the house?"

"Yeah. I asked her a couple times who she was but she

kept saying 'nobody', but she wanted to speak to you. I told her you were getting dressed. I didn't know who she was and I didn't want her to know that I was alone."

"You told her I was there? Getting dressed?" A chill ran down his back. "What did she look like, Meeks?"

"Gorgeous of course, longish black hair, beautiful brown eyes, just a bit shorter than me."

"Fuck!" Mickey yelled.

"What? Did I do something wrong? I'm sorry if I did. Don't be mad at me."

"It's not you, Meeks. Fuck," he repeated. Now he knew why Parker wasn't responding to him. "I'm going to let you go. Have fun shopping," he said before hanging up.

The enormity of the situation hit him. Parker didn't know Meeka. He hadn't told her about Meeka. He knew what this looked like. It looked like he was having an affair with Meeka. Of course, Parker misread the situation. Meeka told her that he was there and he was getting dressed. The more he thought of it, the worse it got. He had to talk to Parker. He had to straighten this out. He was not going to lose her over a misunderstanding.

He dialed her number again. This time his call was blocked. He tried to text her. His text bounced back; number not recognized. He tried her socials, blocked from all of them.

He didn't want to do this but he had no other option. He dialed the number of the only person who could help him.

"Hello," Brynn said.

"Brynn, Mickey Finn here."

"Why am I not surprised, Mickey?" There was an edge to her voice. Mickey expected as much.

"I don't know, Brynn, why are you not surprised?"

"Let me guess. Can I guess, Mickey?" She was angry.

"I don't think you have to guess, Brynn. You know why I'm calling."

"You want to know where she is. You need to talk to her?"

"Yes and yes. Is she at home? Do you think you can get her to call me?"

"Why would I do that?" Mickey didn't respond. Brynn continued, "You told her you loved her but you forgot to tell her that she was only your west coast piece of ass and that you had a different east coast pussy with your name on it." He could hear the venom dripping from her words.

"And that's why I need to speak to her Brynn. This is all a misunderstanding. I need to explain it to her."

"Explain it to me first, Mickey," she demanded.

"Meeka is my cousin. She asked if she could move in with me, but it was just after I went to L.A., I told her she could just live there. I wasn't using the house. I'm staying at a hotel while I'm here."

"You were there, Mickey," Brynn interrupted. "She told Parker you were getting dressed and she was half-naked."

"I know, Brynn, but I wasn't there. Parker scared Meeka. She didn't want Parker to know that she was alone because she didn't know Parker. As far as Meeka knew, Parker could have been some crazy stalker so she told Parker that I was there, getting dressed."

There was a pause. "This is making sense," Brynn said.

"Of course it makes sense. It's true. I need to explain that to her. I love her. I don't want a future without her. Please help me out one more time. She's blocked me and I can't get in touch with her," Mickey was begging and he was not ashamed of it.

"I don't know exactly where she is, Mickey. She's still in the city right now but not for long, she's leaving tomorrow morning."

"Where is she going?"

"On a short European tour."

Mickey had a bad feeling about this. "With who?"

"Colin Columbo."

"Doesn't he have his own band?"

"She's not performing, Mickey. She's just going on the tour. As his guest."

"Motherfucker!" A wave of red rage washed over him. "He's been waiting for this, that bastard!"

"Listen, I'm going to make some calls. See if I can make some arrangements. See if I can get her to call you."

"Thanks, Brynn, I appreciate that."

"No promises, Mickey."

"I know."

"I'm sorry, Mickey."

"Yeah. Me too."

CHAPTER 28
Colin Columbo

Colin walked down the hotel hallway, a bottle of wine and a box of chocolates in his hands. He had just taken a shower after getting to the hotel. He had the rest of the night and tomorrow to himself and he knew what he was going to be doing during that time. Parker was here. Her plane had arrived while he was still in the air on the way here.

He was going to "console" her while she dealt with her broken heart. He hadn't been surprised when she called him a couple days ago, he knew her relationship with that Mickey guy wouldn't last. Parker wasn't made for long term relationships and neither was he. They had consoled each other in the past over broken hearts and he suspected this wouldn't be the last time for either of them.

Was he sad for Parker? Maybe a tiny bit, but he was mostly excited to see his boo. He hadn't been with her for a long time now and he was missing their sex. They always had fun, sex, laughs and companionship. He was going to fuck Mickey out of her system and she would come out of it on the other side a lot happier and they would spend the next six weeks together.

He arrived at her door and knocked, clearing his throat. The door was opened by Saint.

"Saint?" he said uncertainly. "I didn't know you were here. I think I have the wrong room."

"No, brudder," Saint said as he reached out and took the wine and chocolates out of Colin's hands before turning back into the room, "you want to see little Parker, she here. Come in, come."

Colin walked into the room to find it packed. Saint's entourage was there, at least fifteen people, every inch of space on the bed was taken, each chair had an occupant, other people were sitting on the floor. The air was hazy with marijuana smoke and Parker was in the middle of it all with a goofy grin on her face. Some huge guy, who Colin thought had some stupid name like Tiny or Mouse or something, had his arm around Parker's shoulders, talking loudly to the room.

Colin had met Saint a couple of times now. He knew him through Brynn. He recognized some of Saint's posse. Parker knew them all. It suddenly dawned on Colin that there might not be any consoling happening tonight. He was disappointed. So was his dick.

He found a spot to sit on the dresser. Saint had opened the box of chocolates, had taken one and passed it down the line to the next person. He had also opened Colin's bottle of wine, taken a sip and passed that around behind the box of chocolates. Next, he pulled out a spliff, lit it and passed that around. Music was playing, people were talking and laughing. Parker completely ignored him.

$$$

Colin didn't remember going back to his room, but that was where he woke up, still dressed in the same clothes as last night. It was early afternoon. If anything, he was adaptable, he thought as he got out of bed, took a shower, and changed his clothes. Parker should probably be awake by now and, if not, he would join her in bed. Problem solved!

He was congratulating himself on his ingenuity when he knocked on her door half an hour later. This time Tiny/Mouse answered the door. They stood looking at each other, without saying a word. Colin's plans died in front of Tiny/Mouse, who smirked and closed the door in his face.

$$$

He called Parker's room two hours before his concert was scheduled to begin. Someone answered the phone.

"Can I speak to Parker?" he asked.

"Parker, phone for you," the girl said.

"Hello?" Parker said.

"Hey, boo," Colin breathed into the phone. "I haven't had a chance to spend time with you. Are you coming to the concert tonight? I'm leaving for the arena in about half an hour. Do you want to come with?"

"Colin, I'm so sorry. Saint made reservations for dinner and I'm really hungry." She giggled.

"You're stoned," he said.

"Maybe a bit." A moment passed. "But, hey, Saint is leaving tomorrow, I think, or the next day for sure. What day is it?" Parker muffled the phone by putting her hand over the receiver, "Yeah, he's leaving tomorrow, I think…or the next day for sure."

"Okay, so we'll spend time together tomorrow or the next day for sure?"

"Yeah. Did you know that's when Saint's leaving?"

"That's what I hear."

"So…what was the question again?"

"Never mind, Parker." He was annoyed. "You go have dinner and I'll see you whenever."

"Okay, bye." She hung up, obviously not caring that he was annoyed or that she was supposed to be spending time being consoled by him.

But, hey, he was adaptable, Saint was leaving tomorrow, or the day after. There was still plenty of time for consoling.

CHAPTER 29
Mickey

Mickey arrived in Berlin the day after Colin's concert. Colin had another concert tonight, then they were going to Paris. Correction, *Colin* was going to Paris. He and Parker would be doing their own thing. He caught a cab and went to the hotel.

He walked into the lobby and went straight to the desk to get his key. He turned to go to the elevators when he saw a tall, thin Rasta standing nearby. He smiled.

"Saint," he put out his hand, "what are you doing here?"

"She call and send me here," he responded. He took Mickey's hand and pulled him into an embrace.

Mickey knew it was Brynn that had called Saint. "Where is she?" he asked.

"Come," Saint said as they walked to the elevators.

They waited in silence. When the doors opened Colin was leaning against the back wall. His eyes went from Saint to Mickey. "Shit," he said. He pushed off the wall and headed out the elevator.

Mickey stood in front of him, blocking his path,

crowding him. "You better tell me you didn't touch her, you motherfucker," he spat out.

Colin's hands came up, palms out, "No, I didn't touch her," he said. "Thanks to your 'brudder' and his posse, I didn't even get to speak to her." He edged past Mickey, then turned back. "I would have fucked her into next week if it weren't for Saint, and she would have let me," he sneered.

Saint put his arm on Mickey's shoulder. "Come," he said, "let the cock-a-roach go."

Mickey smiled at Saint's words. Colin had heard them. A look of anger slashed across his face and he flipped them off as the elevator doors closed. Mickey laughed at him, which made Colin even angrier.

They went to Parker's room and knocked on the door. A woman answered. She looked past him to Saint, nodded her head, stood aside to let Mickey in, and then left the room, leaving him alone with Parker.

Mickey left his bag at the door and walked down the short hallway into the room. Parker was in bed under the covers, lying on her side, with her hand under her pillow watching TV.

"Was that room service?" she asked.

"What are you watching?"

Parker jerked at the sound of his voice. She pushed her face into her pillow, refusing to look at him. "Go away," she said, her voice muffled.

"I need to speak to you, baby."

She lifted her face out of the pillow. "I don't need to speak to you. Go speak to your girlfriend," she sneered.

"Yeah, about that, Parker, she's not my girlfriend."

"Liar," she screamed as she jumped out of bed, turning to him. "She was in your T-shirt, Mickey. You were getting dressed. Why were you getting dressed in the afternoon when you were supposed to be at work?"

She was mad, but she also looked destroyed. Her hair was a mess, her eyes were bloodshot and she looked like she hadn't changed her clothes for a few days.

"I wasn't there, Parker. I was at work."

"Right, she just got out of bed. She wasn't even dressed."

"She did just get out of bed. She's my cousin. I let her live in the house while I was in L.A." He walked toward her. "She didn't know who you were. She told you I was there because she didn't want you to know she was alone. You scared her."

"Why should I believe you?" Parker demanded.

"Because I am urgently needed at home. Right now, I should be in a meeting with the mayor, but I am here, in Berlin, because my girl needs me to remind her that I love her." He put his hand on her cheek, rubbing little circles with his thumb. Parker leaned into his hand; her eyes hopeful. "If my girl needs me, that's where I will be."

Parker seemed to fall in on herself. She let out a huge sob. Mickey gathered her into his arms. Parker clung to him, crying into his chest.

"I love you too, Mickey. I wanted to surprise you when you came home from work," she hiccoughed.

"You love me too, baby?"

"Yes." She started to sob again. "I thought she was your girlfriend. I thought you were tired of me."

"Tired of you? Never. How many times have I told you that you are perfect?"

"You always say my tits are perfect, not me."

"That's my mistake because, baby, all of you is perfect for me. Every inch of you, inside and out." He kissed the top of her head. "You smell like pot, like you've been bathing in it."

She laughed, "Saint and his people have been spending the last two days with me. I'd be surprised if I smelled like anything else."

$$$

Tony pulled up in front of his house. Mickey helped Parker out of the car and walked to the door with her. He knocked on the door. Meeka opened it.

"Uncle Mickey," she said as she hugged him. "Come in." She stepped aside.

They entered the foyer. "Meeks, this is Parker Chen," he introduced them.

Meeka held out her hand. "Not nobody, it turns out. Hello, Parker."

"Meeka. Sorry I scared you when I let myself in. I didn't know about your arrangement."

"Not a problem, Parker, now that I know who you are and how important you are to Uncle Mickey," she smiled. "Come in," Meeka repeated, "I have a surprise for you."

They walked into the living area. A young man stood in front of the island. Meeka went to him and put her arm around his waist. "This is Carlos," she said. She looked anxiously at Mickey.

"Carlos," Mickey said as he held out his hand. "You took Meeks out for dinner a couple of weeks ago."

Carlos shook his hand and then Parker's. "Yes, that was me. Thank you for that dress, sir."

Mickey lifted his eyebrow at Meeka. She laughed. "It was part of my man trap and I caught him." She beamed at Carlos.

"Yes, she did," Carlos agreed, gazing at Meeka.

CHAPTER 30
Mickey and Parker

Six months later

Parker returned to the table from refreshing her makeup in the ladies' room. She put her bag down as she took her seat. Mickey swiveled in his chair to face her.

"Say yes for me, baby," he said.

"Yes," she responded.

Suddenly the table quieted down. Mickey was treating them to supper. Brynn and Saint were with them, so were Sherilynn, Toby, LeShawn, Marcus, and Silvio.

"Say it again," he said.

"Yes," she smiled.

"Are you happy, baby?" He picked up her hand and held it in his, her palm up.

"Yes."

"You know I love you." He gave her a smouldering look.

"Yes." Her panties were suddenly moist.

"And you love me?"

"Yes."

He placed a small Tiffany's box on her palm and

snapped it open to reveal a large diamond ring. "Say yes, please, baby. Marry me."

She looked at the ring, then at Mickey, then at the ring. "Yes," she replied with no hesitation.

The table cheered and a waiter with a bottle of champagne appeared. Mickey took the ring out of the box and slid it onto her finger. A cork popped. Mickey pulled her onto his lap, pulling her lips up to his.

"There better be a piece of cake for me around here somewhere," she said against his lips.

He made eye contact with the waiter and nodded his head. Three waiters came out of the kitchen each bearing huge trays, all covered with plates of cake.

"I've got you, baby," he said as plates of cake were crammed onto the table. Mickey picked up a fork, took a piece of chocolate cake and brought it to his mouth. Parker put her hand on his and redirected the fork into her mouth.

"What are you having for dessert?" Parker asked.

"You know what I'm having for dessert…and I'm having seconds and thirds."

About Geneva Gordon

Geneva is a hardy Canadian who shares her home with her cat, her son, and the birds and squirrels that she feeds in her backyard. She is an avid reader who has read all genres of fiction and the odd non-fiction book as well. Romance novels are her favorite and she strives to make her readers get involved with her characters: to feel the giddiness of discovery, the tension of desire, to smile, to get that feeling in the pit of your stomach when things don't go well, and to rejoice when the lovers find their way back to each other. She looks forward to sharing her stories with you.

Books by Geneva Gordon

One Task: The Warrior and the King
The Demon You Love (One Task, Book Two)
The King's Treasure (One Task, Book Three)
You Can't Delete You
Say Yes, Baby

Also from Deep Desires Press

You Can't Delete You
Geneva Gordon

Gray is an actor surging in popularity with his big break. Carly is a research assistant for a tabloid TV show.

Given the overlap of their two worlds, they should have met before—indeed, opportunity has presented itself several times—but Carly is worried that actor-Gray will be different from the Gray she knows, and she doesn't want to confront that possible reality.

Gray and Carly met years ago as pre-teens playing online video games. It was a chance meeting and an unlikely friendship, maintained through gaming and online chat, but that friendship remained, even as their worlds evolved and eventually collided.

Despite Carly not wanting to meet the real Gray, fate has other plans and brings them together. Will this online spark between them fan into a flame of passion? Or will it be game over?

Available in ebook and paperback!

www.ingramcontent.com/pod-product-compliance
Lightning Source LLC
Chambersburg PA
CBHW020415180626
46812CB00003B/991